A LEGEND COMES ALIVE

Catelyn had heard the legend of notorious Captain Black, the dashing, daring highwayman who had terrorized the countryside, robbing the rich and mocking the law. She had heard the legend and laughed at it.

Now, however, she was laughing no longer.

In the moonlit garden of the manor, where she had ventured alone out of romantic whim, she now felt the arms of this man around her, and his lips pressing down on hers.

And even more dangerous, not only was she not laughing, she was not struggling, either. . . .

CAPTAIN BLACK

ELIZABETH HEWITT

CAPTAIN BLACK

A SIGNET BOOK

NEW AMERICAN LIBRARY

A DIVISION OF PENGUIN BOOKS USA INC.

For Jack and Nettie Hewitt
In loving memory.

1

Arabella Madoc's pretty, but slightly vapid blue eyes widened, displaying her animated interest in the discussion at hand. "Oh, but I love gothic romances, *beau-père*. They are *so* romantic."

Neither the ethereal blonde nor the remainder of the assembled Madoc family gave indication of finding anything amusing or redundant in this statement. Catelyn Fitzsimon, under the cover of accepting a dish of new peas from her aunt, cast a quick sidelong glance at the dark-haired young man seated beside her, instinctively seeking a response. But Rhys Trefor was speaking to Gwynne Madoc seated to his right and did not appear to notice her. Catelyn suppressed a small sign of disappointment and returned her attention to her plate.

Sir Thomas Madoc was a hearty man who brought that quality to the table and to his opinions. He attacked his plate with good-natured vigor, only pausing between bites to deliver his comment on Arabella's remark. "They are a waste of time, my dear Bella," he said to his daughter-in-law. "And what is worse to my thinking, they put silly notions in young girls' heads." He paused to pour himself another generous glass of wine. "Damme, I read one once, or tried to. All die-away females and gloomy castles, and the adventures . . . pure nonsense."

"Do you think romances put silly notions into my head, Thomas?" said his wife Elizabeth, a woman whose quiet voice and gentle manner belied a strong will and determined character. "I cannot think of a form of literature that I enjoy more thoroughly. It is all very well to tell me that sermons and histories improve my mind, but quite frankly, I think it was improved quite sufficiently in my schoolroom days and now I have earned the right to please myself."

"Of course, of course," Sir Thomas said quickly, for more than a quarter century of marriage had taught him not to court the edge of his wife's tongue. "But you are a mature woman capable of discernment."

"You make it seem as if novels were not quite nice or decent, Papa," said Gwynne Madoc, joining the conversation. She had her mother's gentleness of voice and manner, but she was of a retiring nature and only occasionally offered an unsolicited opinion. "Surely a little escape into a dashing adventure is not so very harmful."

"They are all the crack," said Hu Madoc. "Not only in London, but everywhere, so where can be the harm in them?"

Sir Thomas frowned. "Does popularity also confer respectability on a thing?"

"Generally," said Rhys Trefor with a dry inflection. "Familiarity may eventually breed contempt, but first it breeds acceptance and indifference. A case in point is the dancing of the waltz. Once it was considered shocking, but it is now the most fashionable of dances everywhere, even in the sacred precincts of Almack's. Is this not so, Miss Fitzsimon?"

Catelyn had sat silently, mostly dwelling on her

own thoughts and paying no more than cursory attention to the conversation around her. She started slightly at being addressed. "Oh, everyone waltzes. Only the highest sticklers and provincials cavil at it." She spoke to the company at large, but she saw a faint, sardonic smile form on Trefor's lips.

"You see, Sir Thomas," he said without inflection, "only high sticklers and provincials swim against the stream of fashion."

In spite of his characteristically bland manner of speech, Catelyn was sure she had heard a faint stress on the word "provincial" and that it was meant as a criticism of her. She met his eyes for a brief moment, though, and there was no obvious mockery in them.

Rhys Trefor was the only person at the table not related to the Madoc family. But Arabella had confided to Catelyn that Rhys was expected to offer for Gwynne and that it wanted only his coming into an expected inheritance for him to do so. So it did not surprise Catelyn that he treated Madoc Hall as a second home and felt free to express his opinions as he pleased.

Catelyn did not feel this ease. Though Elizabeth, Lady Madoc, was her father's youngest sister, she had met this aunt only three times in the whole of her life before coming to Madoc, and she had only arrived there three days ago, uninvited and barely announced. Catelyn had seriously displeased her father, a man who did not suffer such things lightly, and the punishment for her crime was banishment from her home and the comfort of her friends, exile in Wales with near strangers.

Catelyn had been presented to the world fully three years ago and she was a poised and self-confident young woman, but she had been assailed with all the

predictable anxieties of being sent off to a strange
place with no sure welcome at the end of her journey.
The only comfort she had was the knowledge that her
Aunt Madoc was something of a family disgrace
herself, having married Sir Thomas against all advice,
preferring love to the grand match her family had
intended for her. Catelyn's crime was not too dissim-
ilar and she could hope that her aunt would not judge
her too harshly. Her experiences with the family that
she knew kept her anxieties to the fore.

But Sir Thomas and Lady Madoc were amiable
people. They had appeared genuinely delighted by her
unexpected visit and had at once made her as
comfortable as it was in their power to do, treating her
as if she had always been an intimate part of their
family circle. Catelyn's own good nature and willingness to be pleased could not but respond to this, yet a
part of her, the part that was used to kindness as a
form of self-interest, remained wary and a little aloof.

Sir Thomas, even with Rhys to point it out to him,
took no apparent offense at Catelyn's remark about
provincials, and Catelyn's little gnaw of anxiety that
he would think her words a poor return for his kindness dissipated. But it put her in no great charity with
Mr. Rhys Trefor.

Sir Thomas continued to argue that romance was
conducive to wasteful fantasy. He was challenged
hotly by his wife, less vociferously by his daughter-in-
law, and suffered an occasional comment from his
only son, Hu, who was named for his illustrious
ancestor, Sir Hu Madoc, who had fought bravely with
the Black Prince.

Catelyn, who loved novels and the thrill of romantic
adventure, thought it prudent to keep her opinions to

herself. But the conversation took a turn that piqued her interest.

"What about the plaguey highwayman?" Sir Thomas countered to his wife's last argument, brandishing a fork for emphasis. "You can't say that there is no harm in a man who has honest citizens stand and deliver. Yet you ladies have made a piece of romantic nonsense out of his common thievery."

"I think that is a bit strong, Thomas," his wife said severely. She signaled for the servants to begin removing the covers. If the argument with her husband reached an impass, she would have the option of withdrawing. "In any case, I see little relation between the adventures of a highwayman and the reading of romantic novels."

"Books are legends written down," Arabella said helpfully. And then she earned an annoyed frown from her mother-in-law by adding, "But it is so much more exciting and romantic to think of a real person such as Captain Black."

"I think Papa may be right though," put in Gwynne. "Captain Black is a rogue who has been romanticized into a hero."

"All women love a rake," said Hu, quoting a popular maxim.

Lady Madoc, feeling besieged by the whole of her family, said roundly, "Do you mean that you blame women for making heroes of scapegraces? Which sex is it that prides itself on its bravado?"

"Do not mistake bravado for bravery, my dear," Sir Thomas said condescendingly. "No man of honor would take to criminal acts for the sake of adventure."

"Robin Hood was a man of honor," Bella said.

"He is just a legend," said her unfeeling husband contemptuously.

"And so is Captain Black a legend," Bella said with a note of triumph. "They say he is a gentleman too, perhaps even a nobleman."

"Stuff and nonsense," said Hu scathingly. "Captain Black is just a title given to any local bravo who takes up the bridle lay."

But Bella was fond of the romantic legend of the gentleman highwayman who had a special kindness for ladies and a heroic sentimentality. "You may laugh if you please, but I am not the only one who believes he exists. Any number of people have actually seen him and described him in exactly the same way."

"Yes, dressed in black and sporting a pistol," Hu said laughing. "You would not think him so romantic and exciting, my love, if you had a pistol next to your head and your pearls torn from your throat."

"A gentleman would never behave so to a lady," Arabella retorted with her own logic.

Sir Thomas struck the table for emphasis. "Exactly my point. A *gentleman* would not do any such thing at all and that is an end to it."

"I quite agree," said Lady Madoc coolly. She stood as she said this and the other women followed suit, leaving the men to their port and brandy.

Catelyn had frankly enjoyed the discussion of the highwayman, for like Arabella, she thought a real hero of even greater interest than a made-up one. She would have liked the discussion to continue. Lady Madoc sensed her disappointment, and entwining Catelyn's arm in her own, she suggested that perhaps Catelyn would like to hear more of the mysterious captain. Catelyn responded eagerly that she would, and her humor restored by her niece's enthusiasm,

Lady Madoc led her up the stairs to the family withdrawing room to regale her with all her memory could conjure up concerning the highwayman.

Rhys Trefor was of the same opinion as the illustrious George Brummell that port was a common beverage better left to merchants and mushrooms, but to please his host, who had a fondness for it, he accepted his glass with a murmur of thanks.

The talk was the usual sort at table after the ladies had left: politics, women, horses, and dogs, in random order. Rhys participated in this as little as he participated in draining the decanter of port. He had no more than a passing interest in politics, he believed that a man's *amours* were of concern to no one but himself, he could not afford the luxury of truly fine horseflesh, and that left only dogs, of which he was quite fond, but which he did not breed for hunting as did Sir Thomas and Hu.

He was not precisely bored, for he dined quite frequently with the Madocs and was well used to this, but he rose with alacrity when Sir Thomas at last suggested that they join the ladies. He was speaking to Sir Thomas as they neared the withdrawing room, but Hu's hand on his shoulder made him turn and Hu swiftly drew him aside in the hall.

"Do you remember that matter we discussed last week?" Hu said in an urgent, stagy whisper.

"We have discussed any number of matters in the last week, Hu," Rhys said.

Hu shook his head impatiently. "No, you know what I mean. The thing you promised to help me with."

There was a faint sardonic lift to Rhys's lips. "I didn't promise, Hu. I said I would think on it."

"You've got to help me, Rhys." His hand clutched at the other man's sleeve. "There isn't anyone else I can trust, and it would be dangerous now for me to be seen in that place."

"Who would see you?" said Rhys practically. "No one ever goes there, especially at night." Then his smile broadened. "Except for a similar purpose that you used it for, and I don't think anyone with a tryst in mind will be looking to accuse you."

"You are quizzing me," Hu said without rancor. "I couldn't risk Bella seeing me go out of the house and head that way, could I? And what if Glynnis comes there to look for me?"

"That doesn't recommend the scheme to me," Rhys said dryly. "I don't want to have to confront your doxy. I don't know why this troubles you so. Most men have mistresses before they have wives; Arabella would not be so naive as to suppose you had not."

"I don't want Bella to know about this." His tone made it clear it was not a point to be argued. "If she saw those things at the gatehouse, it would be a sort of evidence. She'd believe Glynnis."

"She may do that anyway," Rhys pointed out.

"I may be able to convince Glynnis that without that evidence there is no point in going to Bella. In any case, it will hold her off for a time, since that is the ace she is using against me."

"From what you have told me, it isn't all that much to see."

"Yes, but . . ." Hu took a sudden interest in the pattern of the carpet. "Not long before we were married, when Bella was here with her parents on a visit, I took her to the gatehouse to show her the ruin."

He did not go on but Rhys understood. "There was nothing there then for her to see. You're a fool, Hu. If you can't be faithful to Bella, at least have the sense not to carry on your *affaires* on your own doorstep."

Hu shrugged. "It seemed a clever idea at the time. Glynnis was housemaid to the Hedgertons then, so it was convenient to us both. I had only to stroll out in the garden or double back when I went out riding. Never needed an excuse to say where I was."

"And you might have been discovered by Bella or anyone in the family just as conveniently."

"True," Hu admitted without any great show of concern, "but I wasn't. The point is, if you get those things out of there, I can show the place to Glynnis when I meet her tomorrow and she'll see I don't mean to let her have her way in this."

"It may anger her and have the reverse effect."

Hu smiled in a smug way that Rhys found offensive. "Once she sees she can't use that place to hurt me, you can count on me to convince her of her own best interests. Please do this, Rhys. You know I'd do the same for you."

"I would hope you would not have to," Rhys replied. But he agreed to go to the old gatehouse to remove and scatter the trappings that would betray it as a rendezvous. He did it for Hu, for the young men had been friends since their cradle days, but he also did it for Arabella, whose sunny disposition and fragility made him wish to protect her from the painful truth.

When he and Hu finally came into the room, Catelyn, watching them enter, noted that Rhys's expression was set in dour lines. She wondered idly what had occurred after she had left to cause this. Certainly, she had been entertained. Both Lady Madoc and Arabella had imparted to her everything they knew of the infamous Captain Black, each outdoing the other in tales of romantic dash. Lady Madoc, Catelyn assumed, merely enjoyed the stories for their own sake, much as she would a novel, but Arabella listened to the older woman and added her own stories with such obvious relish and wide-eyed delight that it was clear that she could see no scoundrel in the figure of the highwayman, just as her father-in-law could see no romance.

Catelyn supposed that the truth was probably somewhere in the middle. Perhaps the highwayman was a man with some education and above the sort who usually embarked on a life of the High Toby. But if he possessed all the nobility with which he was credited, it seemed incredible that he would ever have taken up such a dishonorable occupation.

Catelyn was seated on a sofa beside Gwynne when, not long after Rhys came into the room, he came over and sat in a chair opposite them. Gwynne had a well-deserved reputation for her skill with a needle and was at work on a tapestry for the main receiving saloon. The work required some concentration and she had taken little part in the ladies' conversation except to occasionally correct an error of memory that amounted to a flight of fancy in the stories of her mother and Arabella. The tapesty was mounted on a frame that stood independently, and when Rhys joined them, she politely put this aside.

"You needn't stop your work for me, Gwynne," he said, smiling.

Gwynne returned his smile, but did not take up her work again. "We have been discussing Captain Black," she told him, "but you will note that we did not begin to do so in a serious way until we left the dining room and now we have stopped as soon as the gentlemen arrived. Some topics are less inflammatory than others in mixed company."

Catelyn was surprised by the dancing laughter in her cousin's eyes. Most of Gwynne's humor was so subtle that she was only just beginning to recognize it.

Rhys had known Gwynne all of his life, for their families were close and they had been all but raised together as brother and sister, and he was familiar with most of her moods and humors. He noted Catelyn's reaction to Gwynne's remark and did not wonder at it. He regarded the two young women without obviously seeming to study them and he could not help contrasting them.

Gwynne Madoc was not a plain young woman, but pretty in an appropriately quiet way. Beside Catelyn, though, who had hair the color of new-minted guineas, eyes a clear, rich blue, and a complexion like delicately tinted porcelain, she appeared at best ordinary. Catelyn's vivacity, quick mind, and sudden smile made Gwynne's serenity seem dullness instead.

In the time since his father's death, Rhys seldom went about socially except to the homes of a few close friends, but in his salad days, before the responsibility of running a barely profitable estate had been thrust upon him, he had enjoyed the pleasures of society and had met and been charmed by a number of young women like Catelyn. He assumed he knew her type well.

She was a beauty with a fortune and a grand name to back her, a pampered and petted creature who was willing to please only as long as she was pleased. Though it was a matter calling for the utmost discretion and potentially damaging to Catelyn's good name, Gwynne had confided to him the reason for

Catelyn's sudden visit and this confirmed his poor opinion of her; it was all of a piece.

"No doubt Miss Fitzsimon finds our highwayman a bit dull," he said. "In London they talk about the adventures of Dick Turpin and Charles Duval, which are not to be matched with those of Captain Black."

Catelyn could not help reading criticism in his words whenever he addressed her. "Yes," she said coolly, "but at least Captain Black is alive. Dick Turpin and Charles Duval have been dead forever and those since have been a fairly predictable lot."

Gwynne shook her head slowly. "Dash is all very well, Cat, but surely you would not at all care to actually have your carriage assaulted. I know I would find it more frightening than exciting."

Though Catelyn did not entirely disagree with this, she thought saying so rather poor-spirited. Rhys did not comment but his expression showed approval, which Catelyn was sure implied disapproval of her. Making an excuse, she rose and went to sit near her aunt, reflecting that it was as well that Gwynne and Rhys were to be married, for they were surely a perfect mating.

2

Country hours were kept at Madoc Hall, and dinner had taken place at an early hour. Rhys left and the Madoc family started for their beds at an hour when the revels of the London Season would only just be getting fashionably under way. Catelyn supposed that if she were at Madoc long enough she would eventually grow accustomed to retiring at what to her seemed barely evening and rising with the sun, but for now, though she did not find rising early overly difficult, she was simply incapable of falling asleep at so early an hour just because it was the custom of the house.

She was even more wakeful than usual that evening, with many thoughts chasing each other in her head. She decided not to even try to sleep so early and dismissed her abigail without even changing. She had brought with her several of her favorite books and a few new ones to while away the long hours of country living, but neither a new novel by a favorite author nor her favorite delight of all, *Pride and Prejudice*, served to divert her. Her thoughts flitted from the present to the past to the evening's discussion of the legendary highwayman.

Normally she had a fair control of her runaway, quicksilver mind, but the past two months of her life had been anything but normal and had given her a great deal to reflect upon.

An only child whose mother had died in giving her birth, she had been raised by her father and her father's other sister, who, also widowed, had come with her own son to live as her brother's housekeeper and hostess. This was by no means a humble arrangement born of financial necessity. The Fitzsimon family, though not themselves enobled, boasted connections with most of the important families in the realm and could equal or surpass the fortunes of most of these. It was an expediency that should have been to the benefit of the motherless child, but this had not been so.

Catelyn never thought of herself as having an unhappy childhood. She never fretted that her family did not love or cherish her as they ought. Philippa Mantery, née Fitzsimon, was a hostess of the rank of Emily Cowper and Sally Jersey, and devoted far more of her time maintaining her position in the *ton* than nurturing Catelyn. But Catelyn saw nothing to cavil at in this; her life was not so very different from the lives of her friends who were also the children of the fashionable.

Yet only three days in the bosom of the Madoc family had taught her that it could be very difficult. She wasn't precisely envious, but she was sad, and not only for herself. Her Aunt Philippa would have been bored to flinders spending her mornings in domestic chores and her evenings engaged in fine needlework, but it was these quiet times that brought the ladies of Madoc Hall together and formed a loving bond. Her father had no great interest in her thoughts or activities, as Sir Thomas had in his children; she knew her father principally from the times when they were together in formal company or when she had been called to his study to face his displeasure for some misdeed.

Catelyn might never have questioned her relationships with those closest to her if it had not been for the events that had ultimately brought her to Madoc and had begun only two months ago. Catelyn was embarking on her fourth season. The fact that she was still unattached was entirely her own choice. She saw no point in marrying just to marry and assumed that her position and fortune gave her the leisure to choose.

But this was not the view of her family and it came as a severe shock to her to discover that her father and aunt had very different plans for her future. Her aunt had simply, even casually, informed her that she was to marry her Cousin Edward. Catelyn was so astounded by this that if she had not known her aunt so well she might have thought it a joke. She and Edward, her aunt's only child, had been raised as brother and sister, and this had not only prevented any romantic feeling from growing between them, but had left Catelyn not especially liking her cousin. She would not have wished to marry him if he had been a prince of the blood.

Her protestations were of no avail. Her father and aunt, having given her three full years since her come-out to make her own choice, felt that they had behaved fairly toward her and no insistence by Catelyn that she would not have him was heeded. The announcement of the betrothal was made without her consent and a wedding was planned for the end of May despite her tearful defiance.

Another young woman might have accepted her fate, but Catelyn was no biddable female. Seeing no other alternative, she planned an elopement with another of her suitors, whom she did not precisely love but with whom she might have passed her days in some contentment. But it had proved impossible to do the thing with both haste and perfect discretion. They were found out almost at once, were caught up and separated and that was the end of her one-chance scheme.

The consequences of this had proved both good and bad. Her Cousin Edward took her in such disgust over the matter that not even the lures of her person and fortune could convince him to have her; this was the good. Her father was in a fury such as Catelyn had never seen before and this was constantly fed by her aunt who animadverted on her morals, character, and sense with unflagging enthusiasm. Catelyn had known that she would be punished; her father meant for the punishment to fit the crime according to his lights. And so she had found herself sent into exile in a strange place with strange people.

Yet it had not proved such a dreadful fate and she could smile now at the fears and anxieties her father's decision had engendered in her. Her aunt had told her she should be ashamed of herself and of the grief she had caused her and her father, but try as she would, she had difficulty feeling anything at all.

Catelyn got up from her chair and began to walk aimlessly around the room. As her thoughts turned away from her own recent past, they returned to the tales she had heard from her Aunt Bess and Arabella. The highwayman might not really exist, but the legend appealed to her and she could not but wonder what it would be like to meet such a man—a proper gentleman by day and a fearless brigand by night. This put her in mind of the dashing young men she had met and the parties and balls at which she had enjoyed their attentions. She felt a sudden pang of longing for the life now denied her and knew she was in danger of succumbing to a bout of self-pity. She quickly decided that she needed something to occupy her besides tracing the perimeter of her room.

One of the attractions of country life was the greater freedom it gave a young unmarried woman. Here she could walk out in the garden or about the estate quite unescorted if she chose. The rococo clock that sat on her mantelpiece told her it was nearing midnight, but gathering up a shawl and lighting a candle from her reading lamp, she ran downstairs to see if a walk about the garden in the night air would succeed in relaxing her.

The garden was illuminated by the light of a nearly full moon. She let herself into it by the french doors in the Gold Saloon, which boasted a terrace leading onto the formal garden. The late April air was brisk but not cold, and it had a rich, sweet smell.

There was sufficient light to make strolling about the paths no hazard but eventually, as she was a brisk walker, she had covered all of these twice, and when she reached the edge of the main path, rather than begin a third tracing, she continued into a less formally laid-out portion of the grounds that led into the surrounding home wood.

As she neared the trees she could see the dim outline of a building and realized that it was probably the old gatehouse, which Arabella had told her was the relic of a much earlier estate that had had quite different boundaries. As Catelyn neared it she saw that it was made of crumbling stone and was not in the least picturesque or ornamental, which made her suppose that family sentiment had allowed it to remain.

One of the many stories Catelyn had heard that night from Arabella had claimed that at one time Captain Black had actually used the gatehouse as a place to lie low when the hue and cry was out for him. Both Lady Madoc and Gwynne had denounced this notion as absurd because of the closeness of the ruin to the house, but Arabella, in telling the story, had shivered as if she quite believed in it.

Catelyn did not actually have the gatehouse in mind as she walked, but her steps gradually took her there. Once she tripped on a stone in her path and nearly fell into a tree, but that was the worst danger she encountered, and the only alarming sound was the distant whicker of a horse, which she assumed came from the paddocks to the south of the wood. The moment she located the doorway, which was more vaguely than exactly defined, she stepped inside without hesitation.

Only a portion of the house still possessed a roof and the moonlight flooded into the room she had entered. It was disappointingly empty except for scattered debris; just four walls, two of which were coming down in places. But another doorway at the end of the room beckoned. This area, though also open to the sky, seemed darker and led to the part of the gatehouse that still had some cover. For the first time Catelyn felt a tiny finger of apprehension touch her spine. Almost as much to prove her fears absurd as out of curiosity, she brushed aside her hesitation and crossed the room to enter the darker portion of the house.

Rhys felt the sleeve of his greatcoat catch on some protrusion in the wall and heard an ominous ripping sound. He extricated himself with a soft curse and entered the dark, hazardous hallway littered with fallen stone and plaster. He wondered absently why anyone would choose such a place for a rendezvous. In addition to its nearness to Madoc, it was dirty, drafty, and with all the rubble lying about, probably dangerous as well.

He wished he had not allowed Hu to involve him in his tawdry affairs, but a friend was a friend and a promise was a promise, and swallowing his distaste, he pushed open the only intact door the gatehouse boasted and stepped inside the room. He could not have said precisely what it was that he had expected to find, but by the light of the moon spilling through the panes of the broken window, he thought the room had very little appearance of an illicit trysting place. It was barren to the point of starkness, having only one chair and a table with a broken leg propped up by a book with only one cover. Behind him, though, he discovered a pallet bed covered with a dusty-looking blanket, which he supposed had been sufficient for the needs of Hu and his paramour.

He looked about him with distaste and set about his task of making the room look unused. He moved the chair out of the room altogether and turned the table end over, casting the ruined book into the hearth. He bent to strip the blanket from the bed but stopped as he heard the sounds of someone approaching.

After a startled moment, he assumed it must be Hu, perhaps deciding after all not to trust the matter to him. But then, quite near the door the footsteps faltered and he heard a gasp that was unquestionably female. He took in his own breath rather sharply and his muscles tensed.

There was only one assumption to make. Glynnis, suspecting that Hu meant to stay her hand, had come to confront him. What she would think when she found him instead, Rhys could not imagine. But it was infinitely better if she did not find him at all. Rhys moved quickly to the window, meaning to climb through, risking the broken glass and wood, but the door opened before he could accomplish this, and just as quickly he moved to the other side of the door, hoping that when she looked into the room and found it empty, she would leave.

But after pausing on the threshold, the woman entered the room. Rhys's eyes were well adjusted to the darkness, but the moonlight only allowed him to make out objects, not to identify detail. Still he knew at once that this was not Glynnis Jones. Glynnis was a Welsh beauty with dark hair and dark eyes that snapped and enticed. Even in the poor light he could tell that this woman was fair-haired. His natural thought at this discovery was that Bella suspected her husband's deception and had come to investigate on her own. He suppressed a groan of dismay. His reluctant promise to help Hu looked to have consequences that he had not foreseen. She started to turn his way and he knew that in a moment she would see him.

Rhys reacted instinctively. He put out a hand and the door swung shut, plunging them into a denser darkness. There was a short, soft gasp from the woman and he heard her move swiftly, but he had the advantage of knowing her position and in two quick strides he had her gathered in his arms from behind and pushed tight against his chest. Movement and even sound were made difficult, if not impossible, for her.

"You needn't be frightened," he said in a throaty whisper. "I shan't harm you if you are very still and make no sound when I let you go."

There was no response from the woman. Still holding her tightly, he moved to a position where he could slip out the door as quickly as possible and, he hoped, be out of this blasted place before she could turn and recognize him. He loosened his hold on her, cautious lest she attempt to attack him or try to prevent him from leaving. He had no doubt of his ability to overpower her should it prove necessary, but he wished to avoid any situation that might lead to recognition.

Before he could make the move to leave, the woman spoke. "Captain Black, I presume?" she said in a voice that was low and relatively steady.

He was so astonished by this that he stood completely still, one hand still on her arm and the other on the handle of the door. Though what she said surprised him, it was her voice that had arrested him. His acquaintance with Catelyn Fitzsimon was short, but her voice held the hint of a rasp that was quite distinctive. Nothing that his quick mind could conjure was equal to explaining why she should be in this place at this hour.

"You are strangely silent, sir," she said, and he marveled at the coolness in her tone. He could not know that she was trembling inside and that her calm was defensive.

Rhys was not inclined to credit Catelyn with gentler qualities. When she was silent, he assumed she was bored; when she smiled at Bella's nonsense, he regarded it as contempt. He knew from her veiled but appraising glance when they had first met that the attraction he had felt toward her beauty was likely reciprocated, but the also knew that when he did not respond to the tentative lures that she had cast him, she had quickly dismissed him as not of much interest.

This was what he had wished, for he had no intention of becoming a spoiled beauty's flirt, yet for reasons he did not bother to examine, he was piqued as well.

An imp of mischief and a streak of romanticism that, though subdued by the practicalities of life, was far from beaten down, made him do what he did next. "Do you find the prospect that I may be Captain Black so unalarming?" he asked in a purring, faintly menacing tone. He removed his hand from the door and placed it lightly on her waist. A deliberate intimacy to make her uncomfortable.

"I think it is far more likely that you are an errant lover waiting for your mistress," she said, still sounding untroubled, but with perhaps a hint of breathlessness.

He laughed softly. "Perhaps I am both."

"Perhaps," she agreed with so little outward concern that he actually felt foolish, and nearly aborted his absurd masquerade. But he had a growing, if reprehensible determination to glean a reaction from her more appropriate to the situation.

"And what are you?" he asked silkily. "Who did you expect to meet here?"

"No one."

"You are come no doubt to examine the ruin by the light of the moon," he said jeeringly.

This was so near to the truth and sounded so absurd when put into words that Catelyn could not help a small laugh, though her heart was beating quickly. But still he misunderstood her. To him her laugh meant only that not even the rogues of their county had the power to upset the cool confidence of the grand Miss Fitzsimon.

Rhys not only liked and sought the company of women on an intellectual level, but he also respected and admired intelligent and independent women. He had never before in his life had the smallest desire to break a woman's spirit, to use his own male power to force a woman to comply with his will. He did not understand why he felt as he did with Catelyn, but he knew that he wanted to ruffle her serenity, which he regarded as arrogance.

Dragging her into the darkest corner of the room, he spun her abruptly and kissed her in the hard way he supposed a desperate man would.

For a moment there was no reaction at all, and then he felt her knees buckle slightly and she began to struggle, but only for a moment before becoming quite limp in his arms. For a horrified moment, he thought he had caused her to faint. Now it was he who was alarmed, for he certainly meant her no real harm. He eased his rough embrace and she surprised him again by springing to life and twisting herself free. In the dark, though, she misjudged her direction, stumbled, and fell backward onto the bed.

She scrambled into a sitting position, breathing audibly. She found her voice, and if it was the satisfaction of knowing that she was shaken that he wanted, this was his.

"If you are going to do the thing," she said with an unmistakable quaver, "please do it quickly and don't hurt me. I haven't any idea who you are and I don't care. I can't lay information against you."

The low melodrama that they had fallen into struck him with its ludicrousness and like Catelyn a few minutes earlier, he could not help but laugh.

Catelyn regarded his shadowed form for a puzzled moment and then stood unhindered. "You do not mean to ravage me?" she asked, both relieved and surprised.

"You almost sound disappointed," he said. "Of course if that is what you want . . ." He made a motion in her direction and she took an incautious step backward and again fell onto the bed.

He laughed again, very softly, and remained in the heaviest shadows of the room. He was rather enjoying himself and wondered how she would report her adventure on the morrow.

It appealed to the darker side of his personality to know that he would have the advantage of her in knowing the truth. Unless, of course, she dared not report it. But if she was expecting a lover, he could not imagine who; she had been in the neighborhood less than a sennight.

"Are you here to meet someone?" he asked brusquely.

"N-no," she said, and then added more steadily: "If you truly mean me no harm, please allow me to leave. I don't suppose you would believe me if I said I would tell no one you are here, but you can get away easily enough. I have no means of preventing you."

"Perhaps," he said icily, slipping into the role of highwayman again. "But you could raise an alarm the moment you returned to the house and I would find half the county on my neck within the hour."

"You could be long gone by then."

"But now," he countered. "I have the advantage as no one but you knows I am in the neighborhood."

Unaware that she did so, Catelyn clutched at the blanket that she sat on. "Then you are Captain Black!"

Rhys laughed quite stagily. "A legend come to life."

"And you *are* a gentleman," she said, but more to herself than to him.

He had continued to speak softly and low in his throat to disguise his voice, but he supposed that she guessed his breeding from his accent. He also supposed, more cynically, that it was what she would wish to believe. He bowed in acknowledgment of her words.

She stood again and actually moved a little nearer to him. She might have attempted to run away from him, but she did not.

"I suppose you are from the hall," he said. "What does bring you here tonight? Have you been hearing tales of my exploits and come here to find a bit of adventure?" He laughed in an unpleasant way. "Well, now you have it. An adventure beyond your imagining. Think what a heroine you will be tomorrow to your friends."

Catelyn let out her breath in something that was perilously close to a snort. "A legend come to life," she said with broad mockery. "You are no more Captain Black than I am. But if you were," she could not keep herself from adding, "you would be more concerned with seeing to your safety and escape than with baiting me. You had better let me go before your mistress comes and finds us together."

"Perhaps we both find ourselves here for that reason and are to be disappointed. Perhaps we should console each other."

He reached for her, but with a deliberate slowness, and she moved back again, this time careful not to trip. At the door she said, "I have no intention of telling anyone of this—not as you would doubtless think, because I dare not, but because it is too stupid and vulgar to be worth mentioning. If you come after me when I leave, I promise you that I shall scream for all I am worth. We are near enough to the house and stables that it needn't be in vain."

She waited for a response but there was none. After

another moment, she felt the foolishness of anticlimax, and with as much dignity as she could muster, she turned and left the room. A sudden surge of belated panic rose in her and she had the desire to run out of the gatehouse. She forced herself to continue to walk, and not only because the littered floor of the ruin made such an action folly.

3

When Catelyn reached the house, she did not immediately go up to her room but sank into a chair in the Gold Saloon. She knew that she had been frightened in the gatehouse, but just how frightened she did not realize until her legs turned to liquid beneath her. She sat there for a number of minutes until her limbs felt like her own again.

Catelyn undressed without ringing for her maid and quickly crawled between the sheets as if she expected to find sleep there. This was impossible, of course; her thoughts were more tumbled now than before she had gone out to the garden. But she recognized her principal emotion. She was excited, almost elated.

It might have been assumed that a young woman who had been a reigning belle of society, who had embarked on an elopement to escape the plottings of her family, who had found herself cast into an alien world, had had adventure enough in her life. But none of these things, good or bad, had ever left her feeling emotionally stimulated, and that was how she felt now. She really did feel like the heroine of a novel, and far from being chastened by the frightening aspects of her encounter with the "highwayman," she was ebullient. Though he had remained deliberately in the shadow, an indeterminate figure, the man she had met had made her heart beat in a way that had little to do with fear, and in a way that no "real" man had ever done before. There were no features for her to recall, but the memory of this man would not readily fade. And in the inner recesses of her heart, she knew beyond any doubt that if she could have lived the experience again, she would have.

Though sleep eluded Catelyn until late in the night, she was still awake at the early hour common to the household and felt no ill effects for the loss of her rest. She had not intended to tell anyone of her meeting with the strange man, but it was too good a story not to share. She meant to tell at least Gwynne and Bella, and while she dressed, she went over in her mind what she would say and how much she dared say.

When she reached the breakfast room, not only did she find the entire family already assembled, but another young man who was strange to her was seated beside Lady Madoc. He looked up when Catelyn entered the room and the smile that touched his lips, even more than his features, told her that he was in some way related to Rhys Trefor.

He had Rhys's dark hair and well-sculpted features, but unlike Rhys's eyes, which were of a blue so dark as to appear violet, his were a light, crisp blue not unlike in hue to Catelyn's own. He was an exceptionally handsome young man, as was Rhys Trefor, but the welcoming smile and open admiration that she read in his expression was pleasant to see after the latter's disapproving indifference. Yet, in spite of this, at the end of her appraisal, she could not but feel that of the two, Rhys was the more attractive man.

He was promptly introduced to her as Laurence

Trefor, the younger brother of Rhys. "I heard Mr. Trefor speak of you only last night," she said. "But I had the impression that you were in London."

"Was," said Laurence succinctly, "at least, until the day before last. Stopped in Cardiff to visit my uncle yesterday, but he don't much care for company, so I'll be descending on Rhys as soon as I eat myself out of my welcome."

"Which means," said Hu with a laugh, "Lord Trefor cast Laurie out of his house without breakfast and he knows that Rhys never has more than coffee prepared for him in the morning when he's living alone at Llanbryth."

"Very true," Laurie agreed, not at all perturbed at this reading of his motives. "Rhys wrote me that Uncle Trefor was failing again, so I thought perhaps he'd gotten over his unreasonable prejudice against his relatives. But no. He let me stay the night, of course, because it was so late when I arrived that he could not do less, but he had that damned starched-up man of his wake me with the birds this morning and *his* coffee wasn't even warm."

"Well, you may always be sure of a warm welcome and warm coffee here, Laurie," said Lady Madoc, smiling indulgently at the young man.

Arabella's eyes danced with mischief and she turned to Catelyn beside her. "You must have a care and keep hold of your heart, Cat. Laurie is a gazetted fortune hunter, you know, and the moment he discovers that you are an heiress, he will give you the full force of his charm, which I promise you is considerable. Had I not already loved my Hu when Laurie and I first came to know each other, I think I might be sitting at a very different table right now." This last was said with an arch glance toward her husband, but he was perusing a copy of the *Sporting News* and paid her no mind at all.

"So should I be sitting at a very different table," said Laurie with some feeling. "The rooms that I have now, just off St. James Square, have only a rickety thing that threatens to turn over at each touch." He settled his features into a musing expression. "Fitzsimon," he said consideringly. "Lord yes! Beau Fitzsimon, of course. Richer than Golden Ball I've heard. Are you his chit?"

"His only chit," Catelyn said dryly.

"You mean you get the lot? No fubsy-faced sisters to share it with or profligate brothers to fling it away in some gaming hell? Good Lord, the thing is as good as settled. Make up your mind to it, Miss Fitzsimon, I mean for you to have me if we have to elope."

A brief uncomfortable silence fell over the company at these words. Laurence could only guess what he had said to cause it, but he quickly took Gwynne's lead when she spoke into the quiet on quite different matters. Breakfast was soon over and Hu and Sir Thomas left for their own pursuits.

The ladies repaired, as was their usual custom, to the morning room. Laurence followed them and was persuaded, without my difficulty, to put off going to Llanbryth for a while so that he might join them in discussing mutual friends and his life in town. Lady Madoc sat a little apart from them at a small desk making up the menus, which she would soon be going over with her housekeeper. Catelyn too did more listening than speaking, as she could hardly discuss people she had yet to meet. But this circumstance was soon to be remedied, as Arabella's next words reminded her.

"Yóu are just in time for the Cardiff Assembly as well, Laurie. Did you plan that?" she asked archly. "You will see when you are there, Cat," she said, addressing Catelyn, "that he is made a great full over for being so handsome."

Laurie lounged comfortably in a wing chair by the windows. His smile was slow. "But not handsome enough to have matchmaking mothers cast their well-dowered daughters in my penniless path."

"You make marriage seem to be only a business proposition," Gwynne chided him.

"I am just practical. It is that when one is poor."

"And it usually is when one is rich," Catelyn said to him. "But then, I think that many people with fortunes would as soon marry people with fortunes of their own. It is certainly safer."

"But most unfair," Laurie protested.

"Would you wish to be wanted only for your purse?" Catelyn asked, her head bowed over the piece of linen she was hemming.

"It isn't much more pleasant to be unwanted because you haven't any." He smiled with a fullness that included his eyes and Catelyn had to admit it was a very charming smile.

"If there is love on both sides, such things cannot signify," Arabella insisted, and for this she received cynical looks from both Laurie and Catelyn.

"Well," said Laurie, "if Uncle Trefor finally sticks his spoon in the wall as he has been threatening to do any time this half-dozen years, I mean to convince Rhys to buy me an annuity out of his inheritance." He rose to leave and added, "If worse comes to worse and I find myself in dun territory, I'll just take the High Toby and give Captain Black some competition."

Catelyn looked up at him sharply at these words,

but his expression gave no sign of a hidden meaning. When he bowed over her hand to say fulsomely how pleased he was to have made her acquaintance, she listened to his voice intently to see if she could recognize in it the voice of the man she had met last night at the gatehouse. She could not, and in any case, she reminded herself that he had not been at Madoc or Llanbryth last night but in Cardiff with his uncle. Or so he said.

After Laurence left, Lady Madoc left also for her daily conference with her housekeeper and cook, and the last restraint to Catelyn's sharing her meeting with the "highwayman" was lifted. But still she hesitated.

When she thought about it in the light of day, it seemed more sordid than romantic. If they had not had that discussion last night about romance and highwaymen, Catelyn would not have imbued the meeting with romantic qualities. She would have assumed at once what she supposed was after all the truth, that she had stumbled on a man waiting in a secluded place for his mistress.

"You seem so pensive, Cat," Bella said, coming to sit beside her on the brocade sofa. "You must be missing your home and friends."

Catelyn smiled at the solicitousness in her tone. Because she had come to them in disgrace, everyone seemed to assume that she was unhappy, but she was not. The alternative, being still in London and preparing to become Edward's wife, would have made her utterly wretched. "No, I don't think that I do; or at least not especially. It is pleasant at times to be away from the things one is too used to."

But Arabella was born and raised in Cardiff, a city not to be compared to London, but possessing a vitality of its own with conveniences and amusements alien to the country, and she had had to adjust to this quieter pace. It had not happened all at once, and she could only suppose that it was breeding that made Catelyn disclaim any homesickness. "But if you were in London now, no doubt you would be calling on your friends, or dressing for some *al fresco* party, or driving off on some exciting expedition. All that we shall do today is ride in the barouche to visit Lady Tremaine who speaks with a lisp and wears nothing but gauzes because someone once likened her to a sprite."

"Truly?" said Catelyn, laughing. "Perhaps I shall plead the migraine. But then I should miss the treat of stopping at the rectory on the way home to take the measurements for the altar cloths that my aunt has pledges us to hem and embroider."

Bella laughed at this nonsense, but Gwynne, only smiling, said in a more serious vein, "You must not feel obliged to accompany us on our little errands if you would rather not; Mama only thinks that like Bella you will be bored if left too much to yourself. But if you would prefer to ride or drive yourself about the estate in the pony cart, or anything else, you need only say so. We shall not take offense, I promise you."

"Oh, I don't mind in the least," Catelyn assured her. "I am looking forward to making the acquaintances of all your friends. Particularly, I am looking forward to the assembly in Cardiff. Fancy driving all the way for a ball. We are so spoiled in Town that a hostess as near as Richmond must make her entertainment something special to lure her friends the distance."

"You must not think that the quarterly assembly in Cardiff is our chief entertainment," said Gwynne.

"We meet frequently at each other's homes for dinner and cards and sometimes even balls as well."

Catelyn finished the piece of linen she was hemming with fine stitches. She snipped off her thread with a little click of her scissors. Her tone when she answered was dry. "I am not entirely a town creature, cousin. Papa has an estate in Kent and smaller holdings in the North Country where we spend several weeks in the summer and late fall. We also make visits to our friends at their country seats fairly frequently."

"Oh, but that is house parties," Bella said. "There are always entertainments planned. This is living in the country and it is not at all the same thing. Nothing of much interest happens here."

Gwynne looked up from her work with some surprise. "Are you so very dull here, Bella? I had no idea of it."

"Oh, no, of course not," Bella hastened to reassure her. "But I have Hu, you see. Catelyn has no romantic interest to amuse her."

Gwynne smiled. "Is that necessary to a woman's contentment?"

"Well, at the least it is a great diversion," Bella insisted. "Don't you agree, Cat? You must have a dozen flirts in London."

"Not half so many," Catelyn said, though this was not true. Despite her reservations, the opportunity to mention her meeting the previous night was too tempting. "Actually," she began quite casually, "I did have something of a romantic diversion last night." She related to them the whole of her adventure, except for the kiss and her later elation.

Gwynne continued with her work, but Bella stilled her needle and listened to her, wide-eyed. "Oh, Cat," she breathed when Catelyn had finished, "you are so brave. I probably should have fainted dead away."

"You, goose," said an unexpected male voice from the doorway, "would have scuttled back to the house the first time a breeze ruffled a bush on the path ahead of you." Unknown to the ladies, Hu had been standing just inside the room for some time, listening to Catelyn's story with interest. "You can't be in the habit of taking midnight strolls in the city, Cousin," he said to Catelyn as he came further into the room. "It is not much wiser to do that here. The country may seem a quieter place to you, but you see now that it has its dangers."

"I don't believe I was in any danger," Catelyn said.

"No?" Hu raised his brows and seated himself next to his sister and directly across from Catelyn. Catelyn had the feeling that he was mildly angry. "I think my father is in the right of it. This Captain Black nonsense is just romantic balderdash. I don't know who the devil you saw out there, but I'll wager he was no highwayman. If he were, I don't think you'd be sitting here now talking about him so sanguinely."

His words seemed to rob her story of its romance and turn it to melodrama. "Have you counted the silver today, Hu," she said tartly. "Perhaps if he did not quite like to abduct my person, he decided to follow me back to the house to seek an easy entry."

Hu snorted derisively. "The only thing he was out to steal was a heart or, failing that, virtue. You may have been luckier than you realize, Cat. Many an incautious serving girl out on her own in a secluded place has found herself roughly tumbled. You are no serving girl, but all cats are gray in the dark."

He seemed to find this humorous, but Gwynne, who

usually regarded her brother with indulgence, exclaimed at it. But she could not help adding, "Hu is right, though. An unprotected woman is at risk even in a quiet place like this."

"*I* think it is the most exciting thing that has ever happened to anyone I know," Arabella said with a daringly defiant glance toward her husband. "The most exciting person I ever met was the Duke of York when he stayed for a day or two with Lady Cordovan, who is a particular friend of my mother." Her tone made it clear that this treat was not to be compared with Catelyn's meeting Captain Black.

Hu was amused by this. "They say that York is the devil with the ladies, but if it was less exciting to meet him, Bel, it was certainly safer. I do not mean to criticize you, Cousin," he then said to Catelyn, "but I think in the future you should do best to take your air at night without going further than the terrace. I think Papa should know of this. The fellow was a trespasser, if nothing worse."

When he left, Catelyn at least, was glad of it. She was feeling deflated. She did not care to make quick judgments of people, but of all the Madocs, she liked her Cousin Hu the least. Hu was doubtless fond of his sister and generally treated her well, and since he had no pressing need of Arabella's fortune, she could not doubt it had been a love match, but he often treated both of them and Catelyn as well in a dismissive way. She also found him at times opinionated and inflexible; his words often had the sound of pronouncements. Yet he was not an unattractive man and could be quite charming when he chose.

Catelyn, who believed in fairness, did admit to herself that at times he put her in mind of her Cousin Edward and that this might well color her opinion of him, but still, she could only wonder what it was in him that both Arabella and Gwynne could find to love as much as they obviously did.

She thought that Bella was much too meek a wife, but she had learned enough about her to guess that this was at least in part defensive. Bella was beautiful and well dowered, but unfortunately had the taint of trade. Although her mother was the daughter of one of the finest Newport families, her father had been a most successful coal merchant. The Madoc family, goodhearted people who did not let such things choose their friends for them, thought nothing of her springing from the merchant class, but Catelyn felt that there was at least a tiny element of gratitude in Bella's attitude toward her husband and she believed that Hu was not above accepting this as his due. This did not endear him to her.

It was Bella who salvaged some of Catelyn's lost pleasure in her meeting with the highwayman. She did not again pick up her work when Hu left and made no attempt to hide her fascination in what Catelyn had told them. She plied Catelyn with questions, and the discussion continued until the ladies went upstairs to change for luncheon and the drive to Lady Tremaine's.

During that drive, Catelyn discovered that Lady Madoc had been apprised of her meeting with the strange man. She did not rail at Catelyn as her Aunt Philippa would have done, but she did reprove Catelyn mildly and extracted a promise that she would not again venture near the gatehouse after dark. Sir Thomas, his wife said, was most upset at the idea of the trespasser using the gatehouse for some purpose of his own.

Catelyn felt quite discomfited at having displeased

her aunt so soon after her arrival and began to wish
in earnest that she had kept her adventure to herself.

4

In fact, Catelyn did not think often of what happened at the old gatehouse in the next two days. Despite Bella's claim that the life of the country was dull compared to that of the city, neighborhood visits, a ride about the estate with Bella and Gwynne, writing letters to her friends in town, and beginning the work on the promised altar cloths kept Catelyn busy and reasonably amused. The anticipation and preparation for their journey to Cardiff and the assembly they would attend occupied any spare time and thoughts.

Cardiff was only some thirty miles from Madoc Hall, but visits, at least for the ladies of the house, were infrequent. The barouche seldom bested ten miles an hour and traveling was thought too costly for casual visits. Most needs were supplied by a small cluster of shops to be found in the much closer village of Taff Wyd, with trips into Cardiff planned only occasionally for shopping or pleasure.

Catelyn, who with her father and aunt traveled a great deal to their various homes and the homes of friends, did not mind the travel and looked forward to seeing the city. It was the custom of the Madocs when attending the Cardiff Assembly to take rooms for the night at that city's largest and most fashionable inn.

Catelyn had hoped that they would arrive early enough for her to see some of the sights and shops of the city, but the proposed early start from Madoc proved to be disorganized and much delayed. When they finally did arrive in Cardiff, Hu and Bella left at once for a visit to her parents, Sir Thomas went off to visit his man of business, and Lady Madoc and Gwynne both declared that they were fatigued by the drive and wished to spend the afternoon resting for the evening ahead.

Catelyn knew that she would not be allowed to go out by herself or even with her maid, so she resigned herself to a dull afternoon. She did not make heavy weather of this, saying that she would be content with a book and a letter she had received that morning but had not yet had time to peruse. But Gwynne sensed her disappointment and suggested that after all they might at least visit the drapers to see if any watered silk was to be had. This was not precisely the occupation that Catelyn had had in mind, but it was better than complete idleness and she agreed.

Catelyn asked Gwynne if Rhys and Laurie might be expected at the assembly, and Gwynne told her that Rhys had little taste for entertainments other than quiet evenings with friends.

"I am surprised he does not find himself a bit dull at times," Catelyn said with a trace of deliberate sarcasm.

Whether Gwynne caught this or not was uncertain; she only smiled slowly. "Rhys has much to occupy him at Llanbryth and he is glad enough to relax in the evenings at Madoc, I think. He had little family and looks upon us that light. I know to me he has always been as much a brother as Hu."

Catelyn thought this an odd light in which to view one's future betrothed, but she did not comment. About an hour later, as they were leaving the drapers enroute to the mantua maker's, Rhys came out of the lending library next door and greeted them warmly.

Gwynne gave him her hand and a welcoming smile. "I'll wager it is your brother's doing that we find you here. He would not like to miss an evening of dancing and cards with his old friends."

"Very true," agreed Rhys. "He persuaded me that I was a very dull fellow to wish to remain at Llanbryth while everyone I know is having great fun here. Besides, I am taking the opportunity to visit my uncle. He is unwell and though he don't wish for my company any more than he does Laurie's, duty requires that I at least make the gesture."

Gwynne nodded approvingly. "It is just like you to behave as you ought even when there is no thanks in it for you."

Catelyn thought it was also probably just like him to need some more serious reason than enjoyment to justify his attendance at the assembly. She agreed with his brother that he was a dull fellow and thought it a very good thing that the woman he was to marry found this no fault. Pursuing these thoughts, she flushed a little when she realized belatedly that he was addressing her.

"And do you like what you have seen of Cardiff, Miss Fitzsimon? It is, of course, no match for London, but it has a grace and peace that the metropolis lacks, at least to my less than impartial way of thinking."

"I am afraid that I have not seen enough of the city to judge, Mr. Trefor," she replied, "as we arrived later than planned and must leave early tomorrow."

"It seems a perfect day for touring the city, Rhys said. "If you would accept me as an escort, I would be glad to show you about."

Catelyn would have been eager to agree, but she knew that Gwynne was tired and had only come out for her sake, so she said nothing and allowed her cousin to answer him.

"That is very kind of you, Rhys," said Gwynne. "I am sure you had quite other plans for the afternoon. To be honest, the travel wearied me and I would as soon lie down on my bed for a time before dressing for tonight, but if Catelyn would not mind my deserting you, there can be no objection to her going with you; you are surely our cousin in fact if not in blood."

Catelyn could not think there would be any impropriety in going about the city with a young man so well known to her family and she readily accepted. Then Gwynne, acting for her mother, asked Rhys and Laurie to dine with them that evening at their inn, which Rhys did not hesitate to accept. After walking Gwynne the short distance back to the inn, he turned to Catelyn and said, "What would you wish to see first?"

"It is your city, you must tell me what is best to see. Shall we walk?" she asked, not quite successfully keeping the dismay from her voice. She had seen no likely carriage nearby, and though not exhausted from the journey, she could not look forward to an afternoon spent walking when she meant to dance until the early hours of the morning.

Rhys nodded briefly and offered her his arm. "Is that an exercise not to your liking?" He kept his tone level, but Catelyn thought she heard a hint of veiled amusement, or worse, contempt. "It is so generally the means for getting about in our neighborhood, that I sometimes forget that others are more used to refinements. But if you prefer, we will take my carriage." They had turned a corner and near to them stood a curricule and pair, not of the most fashionable design but certainly serviceable.

Catelyn was certain he was quizzing her, but the keen, suspicious look she cast him was met by one so bland that she had to wonder if it was not her imagination.

Their conversation as they drove about the city was unexceptional, consisting mostly of his remarks on various landmarks. They had progressed beyond discussion of the weather but were yet nearly strangers. It was not improper for a young woman to drive about with a man in such an open way in a populous area, but Catelyn had the feeling that if they were in a closed carriage at midnight on the loneliest road in Wales, it was unlikely that there would be any risk to her virtue or reputation. He was no more flirtatious than an older brother and Catelyn could not but wonder if this was his usual behavior with her sex—for he did not seem particularly loverlike even with Gwynne—or if it was she alone who held no temptation for him.

During a moment when he was completely absorbed in maneuvering his carriage around a sudden snarl of traffic, Catelyn took the opportunity to appraise him from beneath her lashes. His eyes were sharp and intelligent, his features were clear cut and well formed, his near-black hair had a slight curl that made it fall almost naturally into its windswept style. If Rhys Trefor had had the fortune and town polish to go with his masculine beauty, he might have been one of the great prizes on the Marriage Mart.

Catelyn had to smile at herself for that thought.

There was no doubt that the serious Mr. Trefor would have no ambition at all for such an achievement; doubtless he would not consider it an achievement at all. She supposed that she was a little disappointed in him, not just because his attentions to her were not especially flattering, but because his appearance, which should have been backed with a dashing personality, was deceptive.

Before she could turn her eyes to a more proper study of the road before her, his own eyes glanced her way and she was caught out in her examination. A faint smile—possibly mocking—touched his lips. It was absurd, but she had the uncomfortable feeling that he had read her thoughts.

"I hope you enjoyed our tour," he said in his usual tone, which neither suggested nor commented. "I know it was too hurried and brief, but the time is so short."

"Yes, but I have enjoyed our afternoon very much, and at least I will not return to London totally ignorant of the countryside in which I have stayed." She paused briefly and then said formally, "I must thank you, Mr. Trefor. I am certain that Gwynne was right in saying that you had other plans for this afternoon and it was very kind of you to put them off to do this for me."

He shortened rein as they neared a turn. He glanced her way briefly, but his eyes were veiled. "Ah, yes. I did intend to spend at least an hour engaged in silence with my uncle—he dislikes conversation—and then I thought I might visit my man of business and listen to him tell me how much more the estate draws on my resources than it contributes to them. But I do not at all mind having given up these pleasures for the opportunity to please a cousin of my dear friends."

This was spoken with such deliberate pomposity that Catelyn could only stare at him. He brought his team to a halt in the courtyard of her inn and turned to her. She saw the laughter in his eyes and responded to it with a sudden, wholehearted smile. This was a smile that had made more than one hardhearted fortune hunter completely forget that it was Miss Fitzsimon's fortune that he craved, and Rhys blinked at its brilliance. Then he turned away from her as he gave control of his horses to the ostler. He jumped down from the carriage and helped her to alight, and when she saw his face the laughter was so completely gone that she almost wondered if she had imagined it.

If Catelyn had known him better, or studied to do so, she might have recognized that he was discomposed. When Rhys bowed formally over her hand in leave-taking, he seemed only indifferent, and once again she had the feeling that there was an elusive empathy between them, which some disapproval he felt toward her would not allow to come to fruition.

Catelyn could not understand why this should be so, but it was not a serious enough puzzle to distract her from her pleasure in preparing for the assembly. Unlike Bella and Gwynne, she did not have a new gown for the occasion, but she had the confidence of knowing that what she would wear, a daringly cut gown of white silk shot with silver, was in the very latest mode and made for her by Madame Celeste, the most fashionable of London *modistes*.

Catelyn did not think of herself as a woman who actively sought the admiration of gentlemen, but then her beauty, birth, and fortune made any effort at this unnecessary. Still, she had had to admit to herself, and not without amusement, it did pique her that two very handsome gentlemen of her new acquaintance seemed to take no interest in her at all. Hu, of course, just recently wed to Bella, was gladly excused for his shameful neglect, but Rhys not only appeared to find her charms totally resistible, he had rebuffed her early attempts to flirt with him. While she had most carefully dressed, she did not have the *expressed* wish to dazzle either or both of these young men, but she took what effort she could to look as well as she possibly could.

When she entered the private parlor where the family was dining, she had at least a partial satisfaction. Hu's usual languid expression sharpened considerably and had he not been a gentleman one might have described his slow smile as a leer. Sir Thomas regarded her with admiration, Laurence got up at once from his chair to bow over her hand; only the man toward whom her eyes had gone the moment she had come into the room regarded her with no apparent interest. In fact, after a brief glance when she entered he paid her not the least heed again until after they were seated for dinner.

Catelyn was annoyed, not so much at him as at herself for caring. She was seated at dinner between Laurence, who might not have been quite so attractive as his brother but who more than made up for this with his light and agreeable personality, and Sir Thomas. With Laurie, who lived most of the time in London, she discussed life in that city, mutual interests, and one or two mutual acquaintances.

The ladies followed the usual custom of withdrawing after dinner, but only to refresh themselves for the long night ahead. They quickly rejoined the men and were soon being assisted into the carriage for the short drive to the assembly rooms. The three youngest gentlemen of the party decided to walk the short distance, and only Sir Thomas rode in the carriage with the ladies.

As soon as they were in the ballroom, which was rapidly filling with constant arrivals, Hu drew Rhys off to one side.

"You're the devil of a fellow to try to have a private word with," he said, sounding peevish. "I thought you'd come for a word with me the morning after you went to the gatehouse. You did go there, I suppose?"

"I said I would," Rhys replied. "Have you spoken with Glynnis?"

"No, but I sent her a message telling her that her threats were baseless. I think she'll take the hint."

Rhys sighed. "I suppose you found it necessary to put things in writing? If you were indiscreet, you needn't think I'll burgle her room to get your note back for you."

Hu's brow creased in thought. "No, I think I was careful enough. It would have been best to speak to her in person," he allowed, "but I don't wish us to be seen together."

"It may be late for that," Rhys said dryly, and began to walk away.

But Hu grabbed his arm and pulled him back. "Did you see anyone else about the gatehouse when you were there?"

"Who would I see there?" Rhys asked cautiously. He had not been to Madoc or seen any of the family since that evening, so the fact that he had heard no word of his meeting with Catelyn at the gatehouse did not mean a great deal. It had not been mentioned in any way at dinner.

"You didn't see some other fellow about?"

"No," Rhys replied with perfect truth. "Should I have?"

Hu shrugged. "It may have been earlier than when you were there."

"What the devil are you talking about?" Rhys asked with a very genuine curiosity but not for the obvious reason.

"You haven't heard of our little cousin's adventure? I thought you took her out driving this afternoon; surprised she didn't tell you." He then told his friend a fairly faithful account of Catelyn's meeting with "Captain Black."

Unaccountably, Rhys felt disappointed that Catelyn had told the Madocs of their meeting. There was another point that was far more annoying to him. "This was the same night that you knew I would be at the gatehouse?" he asked. "Didn't you suppose that I might be the man she met?"

"You?" Hu appeared to find this both surprising and amusing. "I know you're the last fellow on earth who'd do such a thing. You would have begged her pardon for startling her and escorted her back to the house. I've been wondering," he added musingly. "It may just be possible that Glynnis was playing me false and having a bit of a game on her own. I'll say she has a damned lot of bottom if she's been using the gatehouse for herself." He then thanked Rhys again for his help and went off in search of some friends who had just entered one of the card rooms.

Rhys remained where he was for a moment or two, replying absently to the greetings of passing friends but making no move to join any of them. He examined Hu's statement that he would be the last man in the world to masquerade as the highwayman, and the more he thought of this, the more his displeasure grew.

Laurie frequently told him that he was turning into a stuffy, dull fellow, but this was usually in response to some request of Laurie's that he had had to deny in the interests of Llanbryth. It did not help his vanity that he felt he had been written off by Catelyn as an insipid country squire, and even though he had, to some extent, been playing up to this image by his scant attention to her, he felt injustly labeled. He did not at all want to admit to himself that perhaps it was becoming the truth. Yet if Laurie and Hu, both of whom had shared the adventures and scrapes of his salad days, had come to think of him in this light, what was he to think of himself?

Rhys's father had died while he was still in school and it was only after his mother's death that he had discovered the true state of his family's finances. The income with which his mother had maintained herself, Laurie, and the house itself had come principally from her jointure and an annuity left to her by her mother, and had died with her. The estate, which had only been showing a narrow profit, suddenly had the burden of further expense and was thrown into near bankruptcy.

For a time Rhys had feared that he would lose Llanbryth, but sacrifice, carefulness, and great deal of hard work had turned the tide. Llanbryth was again profitable, but he kept his hand on all aspects of its management, fearful that the success was fragile. Now he wondered if this dedication to his responsibilities had not wrought a change in his character. He knew that he was more serious-minded than he had been before assuming his inheritance. He knew that social gatherings such as this seemed more a waste of time than a pleasure. He knew that only a very few days ago he had self-righteously rejected the opportunity to engage in a light flirtation with quite the loveliest young woman he had met in years.

He scanned the room until he found Catelyn. She was standing not very far from him with Bella and both were gathering about them an admiring court. His refusal to become one of her court, he told himself, was not incipient stodginess, but good sense. Fashionable beauties collected men the way other people collected snuff-boxes or miniatures. He had neither the time nor the inclination to be her plaything, and unlike his younger brother, he had not the smallest interest in her dowry. If he were successful in securing Llanbryth for future generations, it would not be on the skirts of an heiress.

Still, as he watched her he could not deny her loveliness or the attraction he felt toward her. And this was not merely physical. In spite of his aversion to her way of life and the judgments he had made on her character, he could not help liking her. Their drive that afternoon had taught him that she was quick-witted and had conversation. He had played up his stodginess to discourage her and to amuse himself, and had stepped out of this character only briefly, but he had seen that look of puzzlement followed swiftly by enlightenment before she had dazzled him with that smile and disconcerted *him*.

Rhys watched as Laurie deftly outmaneuvered the entire pack and carried off the prize, leading Catelyn into the first set that was forming. Unless he misread her completely, Catelyn Fitzsimon would be no easy prey for any fortune hunter. There was no doubt that she knew every ploy and pretty speech that brotherhood could come up with, but she smiled at Laurie in that dazzling way and played up to him with her fine eyes. For that one brief moment when she had looked at him so, Rhys had nearly succumbed to her attractions.

"Mama sent me to fetch you," Gwynne said at his elbow, startling him out of his reverie. "She supposed you would not care for the dancing and knows that you dislike gaming, so she has gotten up a table of penny whist with Lady Thomas and Sir Humphrey Bowen."

Penny whist, the game of shabby genteel dowagers and doddards. It required some self-control to keep from snapping at her. "On the contrary, I particularly wish to dance this evening. I was just about to look for you; they are forming a second set."

"Oh, I am already engaged for this set," Gwynne said. "Why don't you sit in for a rubber with Mama and then we may stand up for the dance after this—which will be a cotillion. Do you know the steps for it? It is quite complicated."

"Yes," he replied through nearly clenched teeth. "I think I can contrive to get through it without trodding on the hem of your gown."

"I am sure you shall," Gwynne said, smiling. "But perhaps I should borrow a pin or two to be safe." She then left him to find her partner for the country dance.

Catelyn had already met a number of the closest neighbors to Madoc Hall but their circle of acquaintance was much greater than this and everyone who had any claim to their notice seemed to be present tonight. Faces became barely distinguishable and introductions blurred into one another. But she was enjoying herself thoroughly. If Rhys Trefor found nothing in her to admire, the young gentlemen vied with each other for her attention. She knew it was just that she had the novelty of being unknown to them, but it was pleasant all the same and she scarcely noticed the dark looks she received from one or two young women.

It might, in fact, have been a perfect evening for Catelyn. As the hour approached for supper, she was a bit flushed with her social triumph and the exertions of not sitting out a single dance. At her insistence, she and her current partner left the floor to seek a glass of lemonade, and she entered the anteroom set out for refreshments on the arm of this man and bringing two others in her train.

As soon as they entered the room, a young woman, who earlier that evening had been introduced to her as a Miss Jorwarth, walked over to her. She too trailed two others behind her, but these were of her own sex. "Oh, Miss Fitzsimon," she said, sounding excited. "I cannot credit what I have heard. How remarkably brave you are."

"Am I?" asked Catelyn with puzzled amusement at this effusion.

"If *I* had met Captain Black, I know I should have been quite overcome. Did you not fear for your safety?" There was that something in her tone that implied a fault.

"What exactly is it that you have heard?" Catelyn said coolly, though she knew the answer.

What Miss Jorwarth then repeated to her was a twisted account of Catelyn's meeting with the man at the gatehouse that seemed to put into question both Catelyn's virtue and her sense. At the end of this was the spiteful addendum, "You must not mind my wonderment, Miss Fitzsimon. I fear you will think us provincial, for I am certain Mama would never permit me to go walking about by myself after dark and I fear that I am so poor-spirited that I doubt I would wish to do so."

Before Catelyn could reply to this impertinence, she was bombarded by questions from the other two young women, who had only been waiting their turn to speak. The three gentlemen who had come into the anteroom with her appeared astounded by this information and were nearly as curious as the women.

"I cannot think where you have heard this story," Catelyn countered to give herself a moment to find her composure.

"I was told it by my brother," Miss Jorwarth said sweetly. "It may be possible that I misunderstood him, but I am certain that he said this was told to him by Hu Madoc who is your cousin. Since you are staying with the Madocs he could not but credit the story no matter how astonishing."

Catelyn suppressed a vexed oath. She knew that Hu had been amused by her adventure and supposed that he thought it a good story to entertain his friends. "I did go to the gatehouse to examine the ruin," she said, "and I did discover a man there, but I have no idea of his identity. He may have been Captain Black or he may have been the Prince Regent's valet. I did not stay to converse with him." With this she turned her back on her inquisitors. She smiled on her escort in that special way of hers and asked to be taken back to the ballroom.

Catelyn hoped that this would end the matter, but she soon learned her mistake. Miss Jorwarth and Hu between them did their work well. It seemed to Catelyn that every person that she spoke to for the rest of the night had some comment or question to ask her of her meeting with the highwayman.

There was nothing for it but to accept her unwanted

notoriety and bear with good nature the curiosity of her new acquaintances. It even occurred to her, as she passed from the arms of one eager young man after the next, that the man she had met that night might be one of them. She mentally measured each man against what her senses had perceived of "Captain Black," and she listened closely as each spoke to her to see if she could find in any one of them some hint of the soft drawl of the man she had met at the gatehouse. She did not, of course, but the game itself intrigued her.

It was not until well after midnight that she exchanged conversation with Rhys. She was standing beside Laurie, who had engaged her for the next dance, when Rhys came up to her.

"Ah, Laurie," he said softly. "I have just left Lady Madoc and she informs me that she is getting up another table of penny whist and is needful of a fourth. I told her you would be delighted to make up one of her table."

"The devil you did!" said Laurie indignantly. "Whist for pound points is a slow-top game."

"But they don't have deep basset or faro here," Rhys said sweetly, "so you will have to make do."

"You make do," Laurie advised him. "You're better at doing the pretty with the dowagers than I am, and in any case, I am about to lead Cat into the dance."

Rhys noted the familiarity between them without comment. "I know," he said smoothly, "and that is why I wish to rout you. Be of good heart, dear brother, I might instead have promised you to Miss Collins, who has a squint and spots but ten thousand pounds to recommend her." Without a pause he smiled at Catelyn and said, "May I have the pleasure of leading you into this dance, Miss Fitzsimon? It would appear that my brother must cry off from his engagement to do so."

Catelyn did not object, and in fact was intrigued that he had twice in one day actively sought her company. "Do you dance, Mr. Trefor?" she asked with an appearance of artlessness. "I have been told that you prefer quiet entertainments and assumed you would have no taste for it."

He smiled more completely than she had ever seen him do before. "I need some memories to while away the hours in my dotage," he retorted, and proffered his arm.

Over the laughing protests of Laurence, Rhys led Catelyn onto the floor, aware of the wholly childish satisfaction at having cut out his fashionable brother. He did not dance often, but that did not mean that he did not do it well.

Catelyn was a little surprised at his natural grace and commented on it. He gave her a long look and then thanked her dryly.

"I am only pleased that I have the opportunity to stand up with the most sought-after woman of the evening," he said when, after a brief separation, the dance brought them together again. "Between those who admire your beauty and those who are wishful of hearing of your meeting with the highwayman, I despaired of any hope of it."

"Did you?" she said flatly. Catelyn had hoped he would be the one person who would forebear mentioning the matter. "And of which persuasion do you find yourself, Mr. Trefor?" she asked, casting him an arch glance.

"A little of both."

Catelyn laughed. "Well, if it is the former, it must

be the gown, for you have never given me much notice before, and if it is the latter, I shall tell you what I have been trying to tell everyone else and I hope that you will be the one who will listen.

"I met a strange man at the old gatehouse at Madoc. We exchanged mutual comments of alarm and surprise and we parted. It was quite dark and I did not see him clearly; he may have been Captain Black, or for that matter, he may have been you." She laughed again, and he could only suppose it was at the absurdity of the notion.

His eyes hooded slightly. "You were most fortunate," he said. "It might easily have been a more serious and frightening experience. He might have made advances toward you."

There was something in his tone that made her look at him sharply. "He did not," she said with asperity. She had told no one of that brief embrace and she did not even allow herself to dwell on the memory of it.

"Then it must have been very dark indeed," he said with more lightness. "Or the fellow was rather poor-spirited. One somehow expects something more dashing from a highwayman."

"If he was a highwayman."

"If he was not, then the meeting was rather commonplace."

At this point they were separated again and Catelyn was glad of it. She knew she was being unfair, but she could not help being annoyed with him. She had spent most of the evening playing down the events of that night, but now that he had pointed out to her the ordinariness of it, she felt cheated.

"It was not commonplace to me," she said coolly as soon as they were together again. "I am not in the habit of meeting strange gentlemen in ruins by moon-light."

"Which is no doubt a comfort to your friends," he responded with a return of his usual bland accent. But even the mildness of his tone could not completely rob his words of implied insult.

The dance came to an end with the ladies dropping into a deep curtsy before their partners. Catelyn took his hand to rise and met his eyes squarely. "You don't like me very much, do you, Mr. Trefor?"

"You mistake me, Miss Fitzsimon," he said with a smile she could not read. "I like you very well indeed."

Her partner for the next set was already at her elbow to claim her hand. There was no opportunity to say more, and Rhys bowed over her hand without the additional courtesy of touching it with his lips. Catelyn watched him walk away from her toward the rear of the room for such a long time that the gentle-man at her side became quite peevish and at last demanded her attention.

5

If it was Laurence Trefor's intention to fix his interest with Catelyn, he was not being at all lax in his efforts. He became an even more frequent caller than Rhys, and certainly his attentions to Catelyn were more flattering than Rhys's were to Gwynne. Laurie was charming, attractive, his personality and sense of humor so exactly appealed to Catelyn that she felt something like disappointment that she was not falling in love with him. He did delight her, but that was hardly enough. Catelyn found this mildly worrisome; it made her wonder if her romantic ideals could find no reality. Perhaps there was no man to leave her breathless, whose touch warmed, whose lips could transport. But knowing that it was not reasonable for her to expect to be swept off her feet was one thing; she had to convince herself to lower her standard. During these cogitations the unbidden memory of a dark figure, a soft voice, and a crushing embrace was wont to occur. But that was the stuff of a schoolgirl's reveries, and she firmly banished it from her mind.

Seeing Laurie and Rhys so often together at Madoc gave Catelyn ample opportunity to contrast the brothers. In many ways they were very alike, but the differences that made them individuals, to Catelyn's mind, were more to the discredit of the elder. Compared to Laurie, Rhys seemed a cold man, dampening high spirits with a depressing practicality, possessing more a sense of the absurd than a sense of humor and with no discernible taste for romantic dalliance, which in her circles was considered no more than civilized behavior between the sexes.

Catelyn delivered her opinion of Rhys to Gwynne one day as they were driving the gig into Taff Wyd. Gwynne did not, as Catelyn half expected, jump to his defense. She smiled her gentle smile and said, "You make it sound as if Rhys had no other conversation but pig farming and land reclamation, Cat. That is hardly so. I'll grant you he seems at times a very serious young man, but just now you are contrasting him to Laurie, who is something of a rattle. That difference between them gives Rhys the appearance of a gravity that I assure you he does not possess. You will see this for yourself when you come to know him better."

Catelyn could not agree, but she did not care enough to argue the point. The very next day, however, she visited Llanbryth for the first time and discovered that there were more aspects to Rhys's character than she had thought.

Llanbryth was only a little larger than a manor house, but built on elegant and gracious lines that did credit to the sixteenth-century ancestor who had built it. The gardens were delightful, the small park, laid out with a pleasing symmetry. It was obvious that both money and good taste had worked their magic there, and it was equally clear that the occasional signs of disrepair were of a more recent date. But it was also evident that pains were being taken to keep minor problems from becoming major ones. Catelyn, who was used to thinking of her father's imposing estate in

Kent as little more than a place to spend time between Seasons and the usual round of country visiting, could not help sensing Rhys's love of his home and his pride in ownership, which made him more inclined to spend his income to repair a crumbling wall than to make the trip to London to outfit himself in coats by Weston.

The interior of the house was as elegant as the exterior, but there were threadbare spots on the tapestry-covered chairs and rubbed places on the heavy velvet draperies if one looked closely enough.

Rhys lived a bachelor existence at Llanbryth; there were no near female relatives who might have acted as hostess for him, so his formal entertainments were few. Luncheon, to which they were invited, was a delicious but simple meal followed by a viewing of the greenhouses, which contained a collection of exotic as well as more practical plants. These were as prettily set out and as efficiently maintained as any Catelyn had seen on far larger estates. Everything at Llanbryth reflected to the credit of its owner.

After leaving the greenhouses, the guests drifted about according to their interests. Catelyn had been intrigued by a glimpse of an ancient-looking tapestry hanging in a gallery along the back of the house, and she returned indoors and was conducted up a finely carved staircase by Rhys's housekeeper, a local woman who did not live in the house, but who, with two other maids from the village, came in daily to assist the butler and two footmen.

The tapestry was quite pretty and Catelyn thought it probably represented a visual genealogy of Rhys's mother's family to whom the estate had belonged. When she had had her fill of it, she wandered down to the ground floor again, meaning to go out to the gardens and perhaps find Arabella and Gwynne. But as she passed an open door off the front hall, she was caught by the sight of an unusually constructed musical instrument, which on second glance appeared to be a virginal. She could not resist a closer inspection and opened the instrument, lightly running her fingers over keys and savoring the delicate sound.

Catelyn heard footsteps in the hall and closed the instrument, forcing herself not to do so with guilty haste. As luck would have it, before she could turn away, the master of Llanbryth himself came into the room. Catelyn felt a slightly warming sensation and prayed that no guilty flush put her at a disadvantage.

But his only expression, when he entered the room, was a smile. He saw at once what had caught her interest and said, "It is very pretty, is it not? It belonged to my great-grandmother and I am told that she performed quite proficiently. Mama preferred the pianoforte, so I have never heard it played." He touched it in a caressing way much as Catelyn had done, obviously as affected by its beauty as she had been. "I have heard you play at Madoc, Miss Fitzsimon, and you play well. Could I persuade you to try this for me?"

Used to competing with the best amateurs of the ton, Catelyn was surprised to hear herself so described, and further, was a little surprised that Rhys would notice an accomplishment of hers. "You are generous in your opinion, sir," she said. "I am afraid I would give a poor performance and you would still be denied the beauty of the instrument."

"Even if that were so—and I do not believe it—I would still have the pleasure of watching you play," he said softly. "Will you?"

There was a caressing note in his voice and Catelyn could not help responding to it. She was not sure why, but she very much wished she could acquit herself well on the small keyboard. She felt an unaccustomed anxiety about trying, but she could not refuse him.

The virginal rested on a low table, and when she did not again protest, he took this for assent and moved a delicate, brocaded chair over to it for her. Meeting his eyes for a brief moment, she sat and again opened the instrument, pausing for a moment before touching the keys. She played the refrain from a currently popular ballad which she knew ill-suited both the instrument and the occasion, but which for some vexing reason was the only piece of music she could call to her mind at the moment.

"Very well indeed, Miss Fitzsimon," he said quietly when she was finished.

She rose and looked up at his greater height. "You flatter, sir." There was no flirtation in her tone.

He smiled slowly, and there was mockery in his expression, though she was not sure if it was for her or for himself. "No, Miss Fitzsimon, that won't do. You can't think me dull and prosy at one moment and accuse me of dalliance the next. Unless," he said scrupulously, "you find my attempts at gallantry ponderous."

Catelyn rose and walked around the chair until she stood beside him. "I am not sure what I think of you," she said with a frankness that surprised even her. "I admit I thought I had your measure, but I think perhaps you are more complex than a quick study can decipher."

"You flatter me," he said mockingly, but with a smile in his eyes that robbed it of any offensiveness. He became suddenly serious. "My manner toward you when we were in Cardiff was somewhat unkind. I should apologize for that."

Once again Catelyn felt an odd and somehow elusive sense of being drawn to him. "Should, but won't?" she said quizzingly. "Come, Mr. Trefor. There is no cause for us to be other than honest with each other. You may not, as you said that night, dislike me, but you do not approve of me. Perhaps you think I epitomize the frippery existence that you fear your brother means to waste his life on. Nothing at all in my head but the last ball I attended and the latest fashions."

"I have never doubted that you have a mind, Miss Fitzsimon."

"What you doubt is that I use it, Mr. Trefor."

His smile broadened into a grin. "I would never say that. It is interesting though. I think you are a society fribble and you think I am a dull farmer. I suspect we are both being shortsighted."

"Well, I know that you are," she said provocatively.

He laughed outright, a thing she had not seen him do often. "I suppose I deserved that," he admitted. He offered her his arm to lead her out of the room, but before they reached the door he stopped and turned to her. "I do regard the Madocs as my family. Perhaps you will allow me the familiarity of a cousin and permit me to address you as the Madocs do. A little less formality between us might make for a greater charity in our judgments."

Catelyn readily agreed, and then expressed a desire to see his rose garden before she left, so instead of taking her out the way that she had come into the house, he led her through a long corridor that led to a room he described as his study, which opened directly onto the garden.

"It was originally a drawing room," he told her as they entered the room, "much as the Gold Saloon is at

Madoc, but I entertain so seldom that I thought the beauty of the garden was being lost for having no one to look at it. I therefore appropriated it for myself. Though this is not nearly so fine as that at Madoc, and it has no picturesque ruin to grace the edge of the wood."

"I would not call it picturesque," Catelyn said. "The gatehouse is just a pile of crumbling stone, and I wish I had never thought to explore it."

"You regret meeting the highwayman?"

He sounded surprised and this surprised her. "I did not seek the meeting," she said with a bit of asperity.

"Yet I think you do not regret the romance of the encounter. Aren't slightly dangerous men the romantic ideal?"

With the onset of this discussion, her happier opinion of him rapidly deteriorated. "By this do you mean my ideal?" she asked frostily. "Since I was presented I have met any number of men who might fit that description and I assure you I remain heart-whole. A certain amount of dash is attractive but only a fool would fall in love with someone for that reason alone."

"I was thinking more of fascination than of love."

"The stock-in-trade of the libertine? Do you mean to imply that I could be prey for seduction because a man appealed to my romantic ideals?" She came to a halt and turned to face him, her expression as icy as her voice.

He gave her a long, enigmatic look before replying. "I am only suggesting that where there is excitement, there is danger. It would be foolish not to take care."

She could not accurately read his expression or tone. This disturbed her as much as his words. "I do not think I care for this conversation," she said haughtily.

"I've no wish to offend you, Catelyn," he said without inflection. "It is only advice."

"Really? It sounded like officiousness to me."

"It was not so intended, I assure you."

"Then no doubt it was your address that was at fault," she said coolly, and turned and left him. After a moment she heard him behind her and took a side path. She managed to feel both relieved and disappointed when he did not follow her.

The Madoc family dined alone that evening. Catelyn found the evening unbearably dull and could only suppose it was in contrast to spending the whole of the day in company, even if one member of that company had been more annoying than pleasing. After dinner Sir Thomas, Lady Madoc, Hu, and Arabella sat down to a game of whist while Gwynne watched and commented as she plied her needle. Catelyn might have done similarly, but she felt too restless. She got up and wandered over to a small pianoforte in one corner of the room.

There was music in a small cabinet beside the instrument and she selected a few pieces that she knew well, giving them only half of her thoughts while she played. Inevitably she thought of earlier in the day when she had played the virginal for Rhys, but she was still annoyed with him and pushed this thought from her mind.

Her success in banishing him from her thoughts did not survive the evening. Undressing for bed, she again recalled their conversation and this time she was willing to dwell on the memory. She was still furious that he had dared to suggest that she was a foolish virgin, panting after forbidden delights. Accidentally meeting the highwayman was hardly the same as deliberately designing to do so, and if she had met the man and confronted him instead of behaving in a dangerously missish way, she did not believe she rated criticism for doing so.

The only stupid and ill-advised thing she had done to her mind was to tell others of the meeting. Certainly she had never meant for the story to leave Madoc Hall, and her manner toward Hu since the Cardiff Assembly had been cool.

As soon as her hair was brushed out she dismissed her maid and rose from her dressing table to walk over to the window overlooking the garden. In the distance she could see a darker shadow near the wood and thought it might be the gatehouse. The garden was much darker and more shadowed with the waning of the moon.

She walked back to her dressing table, blew out the lamp, and returned to the window. It was low with a sill wide enough to nearly be a window seat. The night was fine and she opened the window wide, sitting on the sill. Catelyn was certainly not looking for anything in particular, she told herself, but she looked out across the ornamental and flowering bushes with a definite intensity. She caught a movement, or so she thought, near the edge of the garden and her interest was piqued. She stared at the spot for a moment or so and then fancied, but could not be certain, that the motion was repeated.

Even as she looked toward this place her sensible self told her that it was likely some animal strayed from the woods or a breeze.

But Catelyn was not in a humor for sense. She closed the window but did not go to bed. She quickly put on her dressing gown and slippers and padded out into the dark hall.

Fortunately, Madoc Hall was a carefully and sensibly laid out building. There were no oddly twisting corridors to lose herself in the dark. She walked directly and unerringly to the Gold Saloon, boldly opened the doors, and stepped out onto the terrace.

Catelyn examined none of her thoughts as she did this, aware only of her rapidly beating heart and an inner sensation that amounted to compulsion. It really wasn't necessary for her to wonder why the motion in the garden had fascinated her or why she was now, with utter disregard for her safety, moving along the paths in the direction of the wood. When she judged that she had reached the place where she had seen the movement, she paused and then went on for a bit until it was obvious to her that whatever had been there a few minutes earlier was now certainly gone.

The sudden and overwhelming disappointment that overcame her at this realization forced Catelyn to at last think about what she was doing. "The truth is," she said to herself softly, but aloud, "you are exactly the fool that that odious Rhys Trefor takes you for."

With this she turned on her heel, mindless of the gravel that bit sharply through the thin soles of her slippers, and walked back to the house. It was not pleasant for her to think of herself as the foolishly romantic female he had described, but her behavior proved him to be right. She had thought, no, she had hoped, that the motion she had seen in the bushes from her window had been caused by the return of her highwayman.

She had nearly reached the terrace steps when she was arrested by a distinct sound very near to her. This brought her to a dead halt. She stood still, enveloped in the drum of her heartbeat. Then he appeared, separating himself from the shadows, and approached her.

The picture he presented, even in the near darkness, was sufficient to make her marvel. He wore a black greatcoat with a moderate number of capes and on his head an odd soft-looking hat that reminded Catelyn of the cavaliers of the reign of Charles I, the only thing lacking being a jaunty feather. His hands were covered by black gloves, his feet shod in high black boots, and, most arresting of all, across his eyes was drawn a black strip of cloth—a scarf, perhaps—with holes neatly cut into it for his eyes. What light there was seemed to gather in his eyes, making them glitter in an unholy way. He was, in short, a classically splendid highwayman.

The only thing missing was a horse—black too, no doubt—and she could only suppose he did not like to bring it into the garden so close to the house. The very fact that he appeared to be almost a caricature of what he purported to be made the danger seem less real. Her racing pulse began to steady.

"I thought to see you again," he said softly in the same soft drawl he had used before; she could not mistake it. "I knew you'd come."

Catelyn caught her breath. "I-I haven't. Not to see you," she lied.

"Then why are you here?"

This was so unanswerable that she stood dumb while he approached her. The awareness of his close-ness enveloped her, spiced with the anticipation of what he might do next.

"I saw you in the window," he said in a silky voice. "You looked my way and then you were gone; I knew then that you would come to me."

"I never saw you," she said with perfect truth. "I like night air, it helps me to sleep."

"You might have that from your window."

"I prefer it here," she said, beginning to regain her composure. "I do not expect to be molested in my uncle's garden."

"What strange habits you have," he said wonderingly. "You explore ruins at midnight and stroll about the garden when the rest of the house is abed. You should not wonder at what you encounter."

"It is to be expected, I suppose," she agreed in dulcet accents. "Poachers, rats, and the usual vermin of the dark."

He laughed at this, but stopped abruptly, making her wonder if he feared that she would recognize the sound. "You are here," he quizzed her. "What does that make you?"

Catelyn felt a little shiver of emotion and supposed it was caused by his unnerving nearness. "I am not here for you," she insisted. "I have had my exercise and I am going inside the house. If you try to stop me . . ."

"You will scream and we are near enough to the house for that not to be in vain," he said, mocking her.

She glared and then abruptly turned and mounted the steps of the terrace. As she reached the top she felt his hand on her arm, though she had not heard him move behind her. Her instinct was to break free, but she did not. She allowed him to bring her around to face him again. Slowly and deliberately he mounted the last step and stood beside her. Without haste or physical constraint, she was enfolded in his arms. The carefulness of his actions were a taunt; she could have pulled away from him and did not, and he knew this.

He was forcing her to admit that this was where she wished to be.

He bent his head and kissed her, gently at first and then with a growing demand. This time she did not, or perhaps could not, prevent her response. She felt as if her physical being had become amorphous, dissolving and molding to meet the contours of his body. Catelyn knew that she could not allow this to happen, yet she could not find the will to bring it to an end.

It was he who did this. He pulled back and said very, very softly, "Siren." The word was a caress.

"It is not I who molest you," she said unsteadily. She disentangled herself from his arms and moved back from him.

He did not prevent her, but the corners of his mouth lifted sardonically. "Do I mistake you, fair one? I think not. That was no reluctant embrace."

"Do you suppose that I would wish for your advances," she said with a sneer to save face, but it sounded false even to her.

"Come, admit it, beauty. Isn't that why you are here?"

"No," she said forcefully.

The extreme quiet of his voice when he spoke was a deliberate contrast. "You lie, Cat. Even to yourself."

Her lips parted in astonishment at his familiar use of her name. She had not supposed that he would even know it. It made her feel suddenly vulnerable. She moved back, closer to the house. "Who are you?" she said on a breath.

He bowed in a courtly fashion with a sweeping flourish. "Captain Black, as you yourself have said."

"*You* lie."

"It is a fault we share."

There came into the silence of the night the squeak

of an opening window. They both started as if discovery were imminent. "You had better go," she whispered, and quickly made her escape into the house. Once again she shut and locked the door as if she expected him to fly after her and ravish her on the spot.

After a few minutes she ventured to pull back a section of the sheer curtain that covered the door. She looked to the spot where she had seen him last but he had clearly left. Catelyn knew her sudden panic was absurd; if he wished to do her a physical harm, he might have easily done so by now. But it was not really the physical that she feared.

Catelyn did not sleep that night, or if she did, she could not recall any moment of unconsciousness. It seemed to her that she had lain awake the entire night replaying in her mind all that they had said to each other in the garden, and all that she interpreted it to mean.

6

If at the assembly Catelyn had had the vague thought
that the man at the gatehouse was someone she knew,
she was now certain. He knew her name and, more
telling, how she was called by her friends. She could
only conclude that his masquerade was for her benefit,
unless she was to believe that he really was a highwayman, and she did not. The game might have
started as an accident, but last night was most certainly deliberate.

Paradoxically, this both elated and chagrined her.
On the one hand, it meant that this strange attraction
she felt toward him must be mutual, and this was both
exciting and gratifying. On the other, it likely meant
that some man of her acquaintance knew these secret
feelings of hers with the advantage that she could not
know this.

There was one thing she was certain of: she would
not make the Madocs a present of this further adventure. She did wish that she had a confidant, but it was
not the sort of thing that one could share with people
she had known for little more than a month, however
kind and understanding they might be.

Another fairly potent motive for silence was the lack
of discretion in the younger members of the Madoc

household. From something Laurie had said to her, Catelyn knew that both he and Rhys were conversant with the reason she had come to Madoc and the only source of this could have been Hu, Bella, or Gwynne.

At midday, on the day after her second meeting with Captain Black, Laurence called to invite Catelyn to drive out with him in his new curricle, which he had purchased during their recent stay at Cardiff.

"At least, it is not precisely new," he admitted with a grin. "But it is new to me, and not very old in any case. Fellow at the livery stable where I purchased it told me it had gone into a ditch just outside of the city and some fool whipster simply abandoned it."

Catelyn exclaimed at this, expessed herself curious to see his vehicle, but at the same time was not certain she wished to go out with him, for her lack of sleep was catching up with her. But Lady Madoc suggested that if they were going driving they might stop in the village to match some thread for her and execute one or two other small errands. Her aunt seemed pleased and eager to have these tasks done, and Catelyn did not like to disappoint her.

Laurie's groom was charged to await his master's return and Catelyn was handed into the carriage. She commented at once on the fine quality and ultra-fashionableness of the equipage. "It is quite one of the finest I have seen," she said truthfully. "Beau Wynthrop has one much like this, do you think it could have been he who left it behind?"

"I shouldn't think so," said Laurie, amused. "He's certainly rich enough not to have to bother about repairing a carriage, but men of his skill with the ribbons do not easily come to grief in roadside ditches unless they were castaway at the time, and a good whip knows better than to drive in that condition. Nor would any man of sense abandon a vehicle such as this for no better reason than that it was a bit smashed."

Catelyn begged his pardon for her ignorance of the Corinthian set to which he aspired. "But you see," she added in defense of herself, "I have never been particularly close to any gentleman with a taste for sporting pursuits, for my father is not particularly fond of horses and my Cousin Edward prefers to ally himself with the dandies."

"He apes Brummell, Alvanley, Mildmay, and the like, I suppose."

Catelyn smiled for *his* ignorance. "My goodness, no. He thinks them rather dull. He wears shirt points that I am certain must chafe his ears and his neckcloth is usually tied so intricately that one can scarcely see his chin."

"You need only tell me that he has a penchant for red-and-white-striped waistcoats worn with bright yellow unmentionables and hessians with gold tassles and I think I shall have his measure," Laurie said dryly.

"I think you do have it."

They passed through the gates of Madoc and drove onto the road that led into Taff Wyd. Having executed a somewhat intricate turn, Laurie again gave her his attention. "I don't wonder that you did not care to marry him," he said, and as soon as he had, realized his impertinence. "I beg your pardon. I should not have said that."

She touched his arm reassuringly. "We are friends, are we not? It would be silly for you to pretend that you do not know of my wicked past."

He did not reply with the same lightness that she had used. "That is what we are, is it not? Friends?"

She did not understand him. "Why yes. At least I hope so."

"But that is the end of it?"

A tiny frown of puzzlement creased her brow and then cleared. "Yes," she said gently. "Be very honest, Laurie. Are you in love with me?"

"I think that you are the most clever and beautiful woman that I know," he said sincerely. He met her steady gaze for a moment before turning back to the road and found himself compelled to add, "I think we could make an excellent, comfortable match of it, but no, I don't suppose I am any more in love with you than you are with me."

"Then that is that and now we may be comfortable with each other," she said with her delightful smile.

Laurie gave a soft groan. "When you look at me like that, you make me doubt if I don't love you."

"We *shall* love each other, Laurie, as brother and sister. I have never had a brother, except for my Cousin Edward and he never really liked me very much until he took it in his head that he wished to marry me and my fortune. Is it nice to have a brother?"

"That depends. If one must have one, it would be nicer if one was the elder, but if one must be the younger, then one could not have a better elder brother than Rhys." For a moment or two he gave his complete concentration to maneuvering around a slower-moving vehicle without slackening his pace.

"There are times," he went on, "when I am a bit jealous of Rhys for having the effrontery to be born first, but then I think of how little he really has inherited and what he has managed to do with it. I am afraid I should have sold Llanbryth when I learned how things were and used the proceeds to live as well as I could for as long as I could." He made a self-deprecating gesture. "Now you see what a wastrel I am and will think how lucky you are not to be in love with me."

"I don't think that," she said honestly. "There are many young men in your position and with your ambitions who try to live quite high on nothing a year. You recognize your limitations and have the sense to live within them."

"Is that how you see me?" he said with a curious smile. "I am almost sorry to admit that it is true. There seems to be a regrettable streak of common sense in the Trefor blood."

"That is hardly a fault. And you have the style to save it from becoming prosiness."

"Are you thinking that Rhys does not?" he asked shrewdly. "You must not be too hard on him, you know. He had his own pleasures and ambitions before Llanbryth was thrust upon him. He's the best of good fellows, and a better brother to me than I deserve."

Catelyn digested this view of Rhys's character as they entered the main street of the village. She had to admit that her opinion of him seemed to be constantly undergoing change. Yet she could not dismiss her first reading of his character and certainly did not like to admit that she was guilty of hasty judgment of him simply because he had not at once responded to her attempts at flirtation. She could no longer be angry with him for the things he had said to her on the previous day; last night had proved him only too perceptive of *her* character.

The afternoon was one of complete pleasantness for Catelyn as Laurie escorted her to the various shops for her to perform her commissions for her aunt. She was enjoying herself so much that she had quite forgotten her exhaustion and had no great wish for the afternoon to end. She readily agreed to his suggestion that they stop at the village's sole inn for bisquits and lemonade.

They took their refreshment in a quiet corner of the coffee room, and they were about to leave when an elderly woman with a much younger woman and a young man came into the inn. The older woman spied them at once. Catelyn recognized them in a vague way and supposed they had been introduced in Cardiff or at a house she had visited recently.

"Mrs. Sommers," Laurie said helpfully. "I was just saying to Miss Fitzsimon that I was certain we would be bound to meet some of our friends driving out on such a lovely day." This enabled Catelyn to successfully, identify the two women, for she was reasonably certain that the whey-faced younger woman was the older's daughter. "No doubt you remember Mr. Howell from the Cardiff Assembly, Catelyn," he added, turning to Catelyn and thus resolving the last mystery for her.

"I am so glad we meet again, Miss Fitzsimon," Mrs. Sommers said with patent insincerity. "Elvira has told me such an amazing story concerning you that I could not credit it. Or at least I did not until Lady Tremaine herself informed me that she had heard that you had met Captain Black."

The younger woman cast Catelyn a quick, spiteful look through her lashes.

"Yes, it is quite true," Catelyn said with a show of indifference. "But I do not know if he was really Captain Black, only that he labeled himself as such."

"And you came to no harm from him," Mrs.

Sommers said with wonder and that something in her voice that said more clearly than words that she did doubt this.

"Quite," Catelyn said with a false smile of her own.

"Sir Thomas is our magistrate, you know," the obnoxious woman went on. "One would expect that that fact would protect his property at least from marauders."

"There is no reason to believe that the man Miss Fitzsimon met was anything more than a trespasser," Laurie said coolly as he began to draw on his gloves. "It is in any case a small matter and hardly worth Sir Thomas's trouble."

"But surely you have heard?" said Mrs. Sommers.

"Heard what?" asked Catelyn sharply, a sudden fear coming to her that this dreadful woman somehow knew of her meeting with Black last night.

"Mr. Revis Jones, a particular friend of my husband, decided to return home from the assembly instead of spending the night in Cardiff and he was robbed on his way home."

"By Captain Black?" Catelyn asked with far more interest than the occasion called for.

Mrs. Sommers unfortunately affected large, matronly headdresses that accentuated her excessive thinness and her advancing years. The one she was wearing had a profusion of ostrich feathers and as she nodded briskly, they began to bob in an alarming fashion.

But Mr. Howell proved to be a scrupulous man. He managed to tear his eyes away from Catelyn long enough to edit and correct Mrs. Sommers's statement. "Jones doesn't really know who robbed him. He thinks himself it was just footpads because he wasn't on the road proper but actually walking to the stable where he'd put up his carriage."

Mrs. Sommers gave him a withering look. "*I* cannot recall the last time any person of quality was set upon locally. I think it is a *most* remarkable coincidence that it should occur to immediately after this man calling himself Captain Black made himself known to Miss Fitzsimon. Naturally, you were not carrying your reticule or wearing jewels for a walk in the garden, Miss Fitzsimon. You might have had a very different experience if you had."

"Perhaps he was just lurking about hoping for a chance at the silver," Laurie said deadpan, but his eyes flashed briefly at Catelyn and were so brimming with amusement that he nearly overset her gravity. She hastily reminded him of some "engagement" they must attend, and with a few pretty words and a graceful bow, they escaped their inquisitive acquaintances.

"You are properly set in your place, wench," Laurie said, laughing, when he handed her into the carriage. "You may have feared Captain Black had designs on your person, but he was merely consoling himself for the disappointment that you had left your pearls in the house."

"I never suggested that he made advances toward me," she said sharply.

But he was gathering up his reins and did not notice her sudden acuteness. "Didn't he? I should have in his place," he said with a quick grin. He gave his horses the office to start and in a few minutes they were free of the village streets and once again on the road to Madoc.

Partly because they had stopped at the inn and partly because of their encounter with Mrs. Sommers and her train, they were leaving the village much later than they had planned, and the evening shadows began to surround them before they were halfway to Madoc.

Catelyn could only suppose that his comment was innocent. It was apparently a common assumption that encountering a highwayman in a lonely place and without protection must imperil her virtue. Yet the unbidden thought flashed into her head that Laurie might just be her Captain Black. If he were, then he would know for certain that he had attempted to make love to her. He was telling her a story of a wager he had made and won with unusual results and she half listened and half studied him to assure herself that she was being fanciful.

But the thought did not go away and it was furthered by reflection upon Mrs. Sommers's story of her friend being set upon. She did not wish for the thought; she chastised herself for being nonsensical, but it came to her that Laurie, who by his own admission never had a feather to fly with, was able so very soon afterward to purchase this curricle, which even in the circumstances could not have come cheap.

Catelyn knew, though, tht if it had not been for her meeting the night before with the man calling himself Black, she would probably not be thinking such things. It was exactly as Mr. Howell had said. Footpads waiting for any lone walker had simply set upon Jones for his purse.

But if Catelyn did not like to think of Laurie as a thief, she did not so object to the idea that he might be the Captain Black she had met. His intelligence, his wit, his taste for the dashing made him the most likely candidate for the part and Catelyn wondered why she had not thought of him before. She could not imagine why he would go on with the masquerade, but she could not dismiss the idea for only a want of his motive.

He noticed her lengthy silence and asked if she was feeling well.

"Yes," she replied, and added carefully: "Actually I am a bit tired. It was quite late before I was able to get to my bed last night."

"You should have told me," he said solicitously. "We might have left Taff Wyd much earlier for you to rest before dinner."

This was not exactly the response she had expected to her leading words, and though she scanned his features carefully, she could detect no hint of dissembling.

"I enjoyed myself very much," she assured him. "It is only now that I am becoming a trifle weary."

He increased the pace of his pair and remarked that doubtless it was the unusual warmth of the season that made for sleeplessness. If it was an act on his part, Catelyn had to admit it was a very good one. He showed not the smallest sign of discomfort or confusion at her mention of the previous night.

The road they traveled had a number of curves and bends but eventually straightened near the gates of Madoc. They had just negotiated the last curve and Laurie had dropped his hands to give his horses their heads when the sight ahead of them made him unconsciously check their pace again.

He and Catelyn saw it at the same time and exchanged disbelieving glances. Though evening was approaching, the light was far from gone and the evidence of their eyes could not be doubted. A traveling chaise was stopped on the road and a lone man on horseback faced them, the pistol he directed at them clear even at the distance. After his momentary surprise, Laurie once again urged his horses forward. Catelyn had no time to protest and barely enough to catch her breath as they galloped headlong into the scene being played out ahead of them.

They were heard, of course, and the coachman and guard, the passengers of the chaise who stood beside it, and even the highwayman turned to the sound of their approach. All were frozen with the stillness of astonishment. Catelyn half expected the highwayman to shoot his pistol at them, but thankfully, he decided that the numbers were against him. He lowered his pistol, gathered up his reins, and wheeled his horse, galloping down the road with as much speed as he could muster.

Catelyn assumed that this would end the matter, but Laurence sped past the traveling carriage, giving chase to the highwayman. Catelyn herself might possess a taste for adventure, but she had no intention of helping to arrest a desperate bravo with a pistol, and she finally gained her companion's attention firmly shaking his arm. This confused his highbred team and caused the leader to stumble, a dangerous thing at a breakneck pace.

Laurence had no choice but to slow their pace and the man on horseback pulled away from them. "What the devil!" he exclaimed impatiently. "Are you mad, Cat? You've nearly brought us to grief."

"Are *you* mad?" Catelyn asked with asperity. "With the encumbrances of me and this carriage, did you really think to catch him? If you think you may, you need only let me down here and go on."

Laurie looked petulant and disappointed but at her words he smiled ruefully and begged her pardon. "I didn't think of you or the dangers," he admitted. "But if I had thought of you, I might have supposed that you wouldn't object. After the fright the fellow gave you at the gatehouse, I'd think you'd want him taken up in charge."

"Well, I don't want to be the one who does it," she said tartly. "In any case, I don't think this was the same man that I met at the gatehouse."

"How the devil would you know that? You said that it was so dark in the gatehouse that you never got a good look at him and this fellow's face was covered."

"I know," Catelyn said, and because she could not give him a better explanation, added lamely, "I just feel that it was not."

What Laurie said was true. She could not know for certain that the highwayman they had surprised was not the man she had met just last night in the garden. Yet she really did feel that he was not. The man they had encountered today had not worn the costume that Captain Black had worn, a costume in keeping with her expectations of a highwayman. This man had worn a plain brown wool coat with buckskin breeches. A square of faded blue cloth tied below his eyes, with the points hanging down to hide the shape of his face, had disguised his features, and instead of a cavalier's hat, he had worn an old and battered-looking tricorn, which had been stuffed low onto his head to hide most of his hair.

It was unarguable, of course, that Captain Black had several changes of clothes, but she could not believe that the man she saw last night would actually hold up carriages with any less panache.

But Catelyn had no intention of discussing any of this with Laurie, and not wishing to have to explain herself, she diverted him by saying, "Surely those people he robbed must be in distress. Shouldn't we go back to see if we can be of any help to them?"

Since it was impossible for him to follow his inclination, Laurie quickly agreed and they retraced the road to the traveling chaise and its occupants.

In addition to the coachman and guard, there were three women who had been riding inside the carriage. One of these, a middle-aged woman who was plainly dressed and likely a servant was indulging herself in an attack of the vapors, and she was being comforted with limited success by the younger of the two more elegantly dressed women. The elder of the pair was animadverting with some heat on the want of courage in her coachman and guard and only ended her diatribe when the curricle came to a halt beside her.

"Did you catch him, young man?" she said at once to Laurie. Her voice held no tremor or concern and was nearly a command.

"I'm afraid not," Laurie replied, unperturbed. "Are any of you harmed?"

"No," the older woman admitted, somewhat grudgingly, and added with acerbity, "no thanks to anyone but you. Didn't get anything either. We were just out of the carriage when we heard you coming down the road. Are you Madocs' boy? It's been a time since I was in the neighborhood, but I seem to recall that Madoc Hall isn't far from here."

Laurence introduced himself and learned that the parties of the misadventure were distant cousins of the Tremaines who were journeying to Tremaine Castle for an extended visit, which would begin with a betrothal ball for Lady Tremaine's son and the young woman who shyly made her curtsy to them. This young woman had not succumbed to hysterics as had their maid, but she was clearly upset and her voice caught when she spoke as if tears were very near to the surface.

"I thought we should be killed," she said in a watery voice.

"Nonsense," said the older woman, who was her mother. "Betsy, do stop sniveling," she added in an aside to the maid, and then turned to Laurie and Catelyn again. "I do not wish to diminish the fact that you rescued us, Mr. Trefor, but I do not think we were in much danger from that man or that he would have had much from us. The way his hand shook I think he was more frightened than we were and the only thing that truly worried me was that his tremors would set off his pistol."

"Probably a footpad from Cardiff who thought to improve the quality of his crime," Laurie said. "There seems to be a rash of it of late; we were just speaking to friends who told us of someone else being set upon. I wish he had not got away, but at least he did not get your purses and jewels."

"Especially the jewels in the case under the squabs," the young woman blurted out.

Her mother cast her a quelling glance. "That was always unlikely, for only Lady Tremaine knew that we were bringing our finer jewels to wear for the ball and the hiding place is too well concealed to be revealed in a casual inspection."

She then nodded briskly toward Laurie. "Thank you, young man. I hope we shall see you at the ball, if not sooner. Since we have taken no harm except to our sensibilities, I think we had best be on our way, for it will be full dark soon and we still have a way to travel."

She turned and ushered her daughter and maid back

into the carriage, and with a minimum of further fuss, their carriage left.

Laurie and Catelyn stared after them. Laurie shook his head musingly. "I don't envy Ralph Tremaine his future mother-in-law, though the chit's a bit of a treat," he said musingly, and added, suddenly aggrieved, "Dash it, Cat, I know you were right to stop us, but I wish I could have caught up with that fellow. Especially after hearing that Captain Black has feet of clay."

"I don't think you should honor a rank amateur with that title," Catelyn said. "If the man I met was the real thing, then this one could not be, for he would not have behaved so cravenly."

Laurie shrugged and again turned his horse toward Madoc. "Since Black is only a legend, who can say what he is. Whatever the one who impersonates him makes of him, I suppose."

Or what the person who meets him makes of him, Catelyn thought. What did she really know of a man in whose company she had scarcely spent an hour and that illicitly?

When they arrived at Madoc, Lady Madoc invited Laurie in for a late dish of tea and the seed cakes for which her cook was locally famous. He readily agreed, despite the refreshment he had had at the inn and the nearness of the hour to dinner.

Sir Thomas and Arabella joined them, and as soon as they were settled in the Gold Saloon, Laurie and Catelyn shared their adventure. Sir Thomas, as a magistrate who took his duties seriously, was outraged and Lady Madoc declared her sensibilities quite overcome by the thought that such a thing could happen so near to Madoc.

No one seemed to recall Catelyn's meeting with the highwayman at the gatehouse, and Laurie, who did, did not bring the connection to their minds, and for this Catelyn was grateful. But her reprieve was short-lived. As Laurie was rising to leave, Hu, who had just come in from a ride, entered the room and was at once apprised of the incident by his father. Hu made the connection at once.

"I told you that meeting you had with that fellow at the gatehouse was dangerous, Cat," he said in an admonishing tone. "If the fellow has the impudence to ply his trade in the neighborhood, it might be a good thing to set a guard on the grounds at night."

Though Catelyn had no conscious intention of meeting the man who called himself Captain Black again, she knew she did not wish for this. She turned a slight, contemptuous smile on Hu. "The two things are unrelated, Cousin," she said firmly. "You yourself said that robbery was not likely the purpose of the man I met at the gatehouse and this robbery that we witnessed was certainly not that of a professional thief."

"Perhaps that is what makes them related," Hu pointed out maddeningly.

"His own victims thought him a poor creature," Catelyn said acerbically. "The man I met was not so."

Assistance came to her from an unlikely source. "It won't do, you know, to set rumors about the neighborhood that a criminal is hiding amongst us," Sir Thomas said to his son. "It could make people afraid and foolish. I don't want to find myself or any of us shot at when we ride through the home wood or cut across a neighbor's property on the way home from Taff Wyd."

"It isn't too difficult though to find the source of

new rumors about Captain Black being again in the neighborhood," Hu said with a significant glance toward Catelyn.

Catelyn could not believe that Hu, of all people, would say such a thing. "Are you suggesting that it is my fault?"

"You were the one who began the thing with your story of meeting Black at the gatehouse," Hu said.

"But I was not the one who made the entire company at the Cardiff Assembly a present of it," Catelyn said darkly.

Hu gave her an indulgent smile. "You thought it adventure enough to come running to us with it the next morning. I simply paid you the compliment of agreeing with you. It made an excellent story."

"Which you told to all who would listen without any thought of how it would reflect on me," Catelyn said with asperity.

"But Cat," Bella said, intervening before her husband could reply, "we did not think you would mind. I told my Mama and Papa and my aunt and sister who were there when we visited. I didn't know that you wished it kept secret and I'm sure Hu did not either or he would not have told a soul."

Catelyn seriously doubted this, but before she could say so, Lady Madoc spoke. "Nor did I know that you did not wish it told about," she said, adding to the defense of her son. "No doubt it is different when one lives in town, but here we have known most of our friends for the whole of our lives and they are nearly family. It is just natural for us to share all the things that happen to us and to the people we know with each other. You really must not blame Hu."

Catelyn was furious, but she could hardly show it in the present circumstances. She might be related by blood to the Madocs, but she knew that in many ways, she was more of an outsider than Laurie.

She thought her criticism of Hu entirely justified and her reaction to his arrogance mild, but the Madocs had closed ranks on her and she knew from a lifetime of experience with her Aunt Philippa and Edward, who could be counted on to agree absolutely whenever they wished to counter her influence with her father, that fighting was a frustrating waste of time.

So instead of doing this, Catelyn pleaded her tiredness and went up to her room. It was not just an excuse and she thought she really would rest until dinner. She did not ring for her maid, but slipped out of her plaid carriage dress herself. She did not remove her petticoats but put a dressing gown over them and lay down on the bed.

Catelyn had not closed her eyes for more than a few minutes when there was a knock on the door. Without waiting for permission to enter, the door opened and Bella came into the room.

"Are you angry with me too, Cat?" She looked like a puppy unsure of her welcome.

Catelyn sat up and beckoned her to come over beside her. "Of course I am not angry with you. Perhaps you and Gwynne are right and I should not even be so with Hu. It is just that sometimes Hu can be rather condescending and that does set up my back."

"Oh, I know," Bella said quickly. "Hu can be quite smug at times, and I cannot always like it either, but you see, I love him and it is not so very difficult to forgive."

"I think Hu is most lucky to have you for his wife," Catelyn said. "And Gwynne too is very good to him. I suppose I am less sympathetic because I have no brother and have yet to lose my heart to any man. When that happens I daresay I shall be the most doting of the lot."

Bella smiled, dimpling prettily. "You are not at all like me, or even Gwynne for that matter. I don't think you would coddle any man."

"You make me sound quite cold hearted!"

"No, I think that it is just that where Hu is concerned, Gwynne and I are too soft hearted. But were you loved, I think you would love with your head as well as your heart."

Catelyn laughed and said self-mockingly, "That still makes me sound a mite cool, but you may be right, for I have never yet fallen head over heels for any man."

"Perhaps you are just more discriminating."

"Do you mean more so than you?" said Catelyn, surprised. "From what you have told me, you are not sorry for the choice you have made."

"No, but there are times . . . Hu told me that you are well dowered too. You must understand the gnawings to which I am at times prey." Bella's eyes had gone quite round and she blinked as if to stem tears.

Catelyn took her hand in a gesture of comfort. She did know the insecurities that plagued heiresses. "You must not think that it is your money that Hu cares for, Bella," she said, hoping that she did not sound insincere. "I do not know Sir Thomas's financial state, but I should say from what I have observed that at the least he is comfortable, and as Hu is the only son, Madoc will be his one day. Surely he needn't have hung out for a rich wife."

"Hu likes fine things and a certain amount of independence from his father," Bella said ruefully. "What he wants most now is a house in Cardiff so that we needn't always be under his parents' charge." She sighed. "Sometimes I think that Hu simply enjoys *wanting* things; if we had the house in Cardiff, he would be longing for a hunting box in Leicestershire or some such thing. "I suppose we all have fantasies and wish for things we can't or shouldn't have."

Bella smiled suddenly and reached over to hug Catelyn, thanking her for listening and understanding. "I am glad we are becoming friends," she said with a shy smile, "though we are so different. I only wish for adventures; you have them."

"Oh, goodness," Catelyn said, laughing, "please don't begin thinking like Hu that I court adventure to puff up my consequences."

"No," Arabella said seriously, not responding to the lightness in Catelyn's tone. "You have adventures because you are not afraid to meet those that come your way. One cannot experience what one refuses to see."

"I expect it is more comfortable that way," Catelyn said gently.

"Yes." Arabella stood to leave, and when she spoke her voice was a little brusque. "I had better dress if the Selbys are coming to dinner tonight." But her humor could never be heavy for long. Her pretty dimpled smile appeared. "Corissa Selby had her cap set at Hu before we were married and I don't mean to let her have an advantage even now."

When Bella had left, Catelyn lay down again, but she could not help thinking of the things Bella had said about being open to the experiences of life, though she did not see how coming upon the highwayman on the road from Taff Wyd had anything to do with this. Her meeting with Captain Black was another matter, though, and this led her to muse on what Bella had said about everyone wanting things they couldn't or shouldn't have. It was quite inevitable that she should apply this to her own mixed feelings toward the man who called himself Captain Black and who might or might not be a highwayman in fact.

7

The dinner with the Selbys was even more boring than Catelyn had supposed it would be and she had supposed it would be very boring indeed. Mr. Selby had no conversation but horses and dogs, Mrs. Selby cared for nothing but gossiping about her neighbors, and Arabella's rival, Corissa, was simply insipid.

But tonight the chief topic of conversation was the attempted robbery that afternoon, with Mrs. Selby insisting on linking it to Mrs. Sommer's story of her friend's misfortune. Catelyn responded to questions about her part in the narrative as shortly as she could while still remaining civil, and bore with what grace she could Hu's insinuation that Captain Black was once again in the neighborhood.

The best thing about the dinner was that it was relatively short and the evening ended early. Catelyn went at once to her room, certain that she would at last find the sleep that had so long eluded her, but she was overtired and restless.

One advantage to the busyness of her day was that she had had little time to dwell on her meeting the night before with Black. Or perhaps, she thought sardonically, after being wakeful an entire night thinking of him, there were simply no thoughts on the subject left to her. Of course this was not so, as she quickly discovered. She tried to banish him from her mind, but could not make the effort this needed.

Catelyn understood herself well enough to know that it was largely the forbidden aspect of their meetings, his boldness in daring to make love to her, that stirred the desire she could not help feeling.

Catelyn also sensed something more that attracted her to this man; a strength of character, the assurance of a man who knew what he wanted, a quick mind that complimented her own quicksilver personality, and the flashes of dry, mocking humor all held strong appeal for her.

The truth was that in spite of the excitement of the masquerade, in spite of the stimulation of the game, she was beginning to wish that it would end and that she could know the real identity of the man who called himself Black. It had occurred to her, though, that perhaps there was more to his disguise than an agreeable game. It might be a necessity. Not necessarily because he was a criminal who dared not reveal himself, but because of the encumbrance of a wife and a filling nursery.

She very much feared these speculations becoming a full-time occupation and decided to rid herself of her fascination by avoiding him if he returned. But she immediately convinced herself that it would be best to meet him again to see if she could discover his identity. The more she thought, the more certain she was that she *must* know this man. And the more she thought of this, the more she was determined *to* know him.

Sleep did at last overtake her, but the very next night she dismissed her abigail and took up her vigil at the window. The time passed slowly. She did not even know for certain that he would ever come to her again.

Catelyn was resonably comfortable, settled on the pillows she had placed around her. She did not realize her tiredness until she started with the motion of her head nodding forward and realized that she was drifting into sleep. There was not enough moonlight for her to see the mantel clock in the shadows of the room, but her legs were cramped and her lower back ached and she could easily guess that the hour was well advanced. Giving it up, she returned to bed but kept her vigil the following night and the night after that as well. If Black paid any surreptitious visits to the garden in that time, she had no sign of it.

She was far more disappointed than the occasion warranted and this made her angry with herself. She scorned Bella's claim that she was different from her or Gwynne and roundly told herself that if anything, she was more foolish and besotted of a man than either of these. And this was what troubled her most; her longings and sense of disappointment were those of a woman in the throes of love, and since she could not believe herself in love with a man she had met twice and whose name she did not even know, this could only be a green girl's infatuation, which she found thoroughly degrading.

By the end of the third evening, she knew that the only way she would find peace was to forget his existence and never again look for him, but the next night, when the house was still and her candle extinguished, she once again was in her window.

The next day she was determined not to give in to what she thought of as her weaker self, and this resolve was aided by the uselessness of her recent vigils.

The presence of Laurie at dinner provided some

diversion for her that night. Rhys too had been invited, but a prior engagement forced him to refuse, though he promised to stop at Madoc Hall on his return to Llanbryth to share tea with the ladies, or as was more likely, a tumbler of brandy with his brother and the Madoc men after the women had retired. The evening passed pleasantly enough, though Catelyn could not entirely help being distracted.

Laurie, a fairly astute young man, did not fail to note this. "Are you still having trouble sleeping?" he asked, coming to stand beside her at the pianoforte to which she had wandered, as she often did after dinner.

Catelyn was absently moving her fingers over the keys, playing bits of popular songs as they came into her head. Laurie lowered himself beside her on the bench and began, with surprising ability, to add impromptu harmonies to her simple notes. She began to play more seriously and he followed her lead. Convinced after several minutes of this that his talent surpassed her own, she gave it up and left him in possession of the keyboard. He flashed her an echanting smile. "I think we have many interests in common. More and more I become convinced that I should make violent love to you to press my suit."

"I thought we agreed to a permanently platonic relationship," she said. "Besides, you keep telling me that you mean to pay your addresses to me for my fortune if not for my person, but you don't really do it, do you?"

He laughed. "I'm afraid I'm a dead loss at heiress hunting. It is not that they do not come into my ken, but . . ."

"You want something warmer than gold guineas for a bedfellow," said a familiar voice behind them, and they both turned to find Rhys.

"I would not have put it so crudely," Laurie chided, "but, yes. That is the truth of it."

"Almost I have hope for you Laurie," said his brother. "There is more to life than being put up for the Four Horse Club."

"Ah, but compared to that, is it worth having?"

Catelyn did not enter into their banter but rose, and pleading the excuse of her sleeplessness, which Laurie had conveniently suggested for her, she excused herself. Not, she told herself firmly, to pursue her endless thoughts on Captain Black, but to get the rest she had futilely lost the past four nights.

But she was not really so very tired, and almost like metal to a magnet she felt drawn to the Gold Saloon. It was far too early for any hope of meeting the highwayman, willingly or unwillingly, and she opened the garden doors and stepped out onto the terrace. She heard a sound behind her and turned to find a man standing in the doorway. She recognized Rhys at once, but the very presence of a man in this place at night was enough to make her inhale sharply.

"I beg your pardon, Catelyn," he said softly, "I did not mean to startle you."

"I thought I was alone," she said.

"Do you wish to be? Is it because of me that you left Laurie so abruptly just now."

"No, of course not."

"Are you still out of charity with me?"

"For what you said to me the other day?" She sighed softly. "No, not anymore." She could not, of course, tell him that it was because he had been proven right.

He stepped out of the doorway onto the terrace. "I have thought about what you said to me that day. Perhaps I have become dull and prosy and no longer have any address. I don't think it was always so, but I seem to have forgotten how to charm."

A low balustrade encircled most of the terrace; he walked past her and sat on the edge of this, looking out onto the garden. She came over and sat beside him. "It isn't true; you aren't those things. I admit that I thought so when we first met, but it was my judgment that was at fault and not your character. And I think I became so angry with you that day at Llanbryth because you said things I didn't wish to hear. Romantic folly can be a dangerous thing."

"But attractive."

"Yes," she said, nodding, "and also ephemeral. Which is just as well, I expect," she added with a short laugh. "Breathlessness and a fluttering pulse are wearing to sustain."

"Then there is hope," he said very quietly, and turned to face her. Puzzled, she asked him to repeat his words. "I said, I should hope so," he replied. "Which will now condemn me as hopelessly unromantic. I too have been guilty of hasty judgments," he added. "You like it here, don't you?"

"Yes, very much. I admit I thought I would hate it and be perfectly wretched until I could get back to London and my friends."

"But you don't?" he asked leadingly.

"I would be lying to you if I said that I *never* think of my friends," she said. For some reason she found it very easy to say what was really in her mind and heart to this man. She did not pause to examine why this should be.

"The other day," she went on, "I became angry at Hu because he told all of his friends about the night I met Captain Black in the gatehouse. Aunt Bess said I should not mind because they were used to telling everyone nearly everything because it was as if the whole neighborhood were kin to each other. I've never known that before and I like it very much. It makes one feel as if one really belongs."

"Don't you feel as if you belong in your home with your father?"

Catelyn shook her head, though not precisely to mean that she did not. "It is not the same thing," she said, her voice sounding a bit constricted. She stood and walked the length of the terrace to the other side.

"I think perhaps I owe you an apology, Cat," he said, rising also and crossing to stand beside her. "My judgment of you has been at fault too."

She shook her head again. "Not as much as you may think."

"What do you mean?"

"I *am* just a spoiled heiress with a taste for romantic folly." She turned her head away from him, for her eyes had filled suddenly with tears that had to be held back.

"No," he said softly, "*You* are none of *those* things." He reached out to touch her and began to say, "Cat, there is something I must tell you. . . ." But he never completed the motion or the thought. She turned to him and even in the dim light of the waxing moon, he could see from her expression that the time for shared confidences was over.

"So now we think better of each other," she said lightly. "Which is much more comfortable than being determined to dislike each other. We are neither of us very good at first impressions, are we? Do you know when I first met Laurie I was certain I would develop a *tendre* for him, but instead we have become like brother and sister. It was the same with Bella. I thought she had what my Cousin Edward would call more hair than wit, but her understanding is not at all inferior."

"We should both of us be more careful in our judgments," he agreed with a return to his usual bland tone. "I had no idea, for example, that it was Hu who told everyone of your meeting with the highwayman."

"Do you mean you thought that I had done so," she said, surprised.

"It is a common trick of your sex, is it not? To figure in a romantic situation as the heroine draws the commiseration of one sex and the admiration of the other?"

Catelyn did not know whether she was insulted or amused. "Did you think I courted the meeting with the highwayman to make myself important? Good heavens, sir, what behavior of mine since that time has made you alter your opinion of me?"

"You put meaning into my words that I did not intend," he complained.

"I think that in spite of admitting that our first impressions of each other were erroneous, we still do not understand each other very well." Her voice had become cool. She held out her hand to him in leave-taking. "Perhaps we should agree to disagree. Will you excuse me, Rhys? I had best go to my room as I told my aunt I would; she may look for me and wonder where I have gone." She did not wait for his reply but turned quickly and left him.

Though his absense would be noted, Rhys did not at once return to the drawing room. He had so nearly told her the truth. What would she think, what would she say if she knew that he was Captain Black? He had been teasing himself with that question since the day of her visit to Llanbryth and increasingly he knew that he had to have the answer.

Rhys had been powerfully attracted to Catelyn almost from the time they had met but he had never believed that he would come to feel as he did now, almost possessed by that attraction. He wanted her, and much more, he needed her; she was becoming necessary to his happiness and this both elated and frightened him. She was not at all the kind of woman he had meant to fall in love with.

He smiled at himself for this thought. It was a woman such as Gwynne, of placid temperment and biddable nature that he had thought he would one day love, not a woman whose smile dazzled, whose vivaciousness charmed, whose laughing eyes enchanted. But Gwynne or women of her ilk never stirred anything but brotherly feelings in him. The feeling he had for Catelyn was unlike any he had known before, and despite his sensible self, which told him that she was not the woman for him, he was finding it almost impossible to keep his desire for her in check.

Where these feelings would lead him he had no idea; until now his masquerade as Captain Black had at least allowed him to take her in his arms with impunity, but it couldn't go on much longer and he knew it. He breathed deeply of the seductive night air and made a resolution. It was not a punctilious resolution but the only one he could make that would satisfy the man in him what was Captain Black as well the conventional upright owner of Llanbryth.

Catelyn hastened to her room, more upset than

before. Her coolness to Rhys had been deliberate; she had known at that moment that she did not want to be on good terms with him, or rather did not dare.

What was the matter with her? she demanded of herself savagely. Out of all the men she had met since her presentation, out of all the men who had courted her, the only two she could find to awaken a genuine response in her were a highwayman and the man who would one day be betrothed to her Cousin Gwynne. As she had sat so close beside him, confiding things she had not yet even examined in her own heart, she had become increasingly aware of him as a man. When she had spoken of belonging, she had had the sudden wish to belong to him. If he had taken her in his arms at that moment, she would not have scorned his embrace. In fact she very much feared that she would have responded with fervor.

She got up from the chair into which she had cast herself and rang for her maid. She had had quite enough thoughts to disturb her peace in the last few days; she meant to be self-disciplined and put both impossible men from her mind, and at least for this night to get the rest she so needed.

Catelyn did not so much as allow herself to glance in the direction of the windows above the garden. She decided she would keep her thoughts on improving topics only, and accordingly, whenever she would slide into unwanted thoughts of Rhys or Captain Black, she was very firm with herself and again returned her mind to Mrs. Hubbard's "Ten Golden Rules of Housewifery." But the truth was that nearly an hour passed in this occupation and only eight rules were recalled. Almost, almost, she was tempted to give in to her worse self in the hope that she might finally find sleep.

When she first heard the noise, she suspected it was just one of those indefinable sounds one thinks one hears between awaking and sleeping. But she knew she was quite awake. She concentrated on the noise, should it come again, and she was rewarded.

It took only a moment to identify. It was something, dirt or stones most likely, striking the windowpanes. Her heart began to beat faster.

She wanted to ignore it, to bury herself deeper beneath the sheets, but could not. Almost angry with herself for her want of self-control, she abruptly tossed aside the sheet that covered her and climbed out of bed. She found her slippers and dressing gown without bothering to light a candle.

Reaching the Gold Saloon, she did have a moment of hesitation before opening the door. What if he really was the same man who had held up the carriage? But the lure was more than she could resist. He was sitting on the balustrade in almost the exact position that Rhys had occupied only an hour or so before, but she was facing the house not the garden, and when he saw her he stood. He was dressed as before, in the classic costume of a highwayman and Catelyn found this somehow reassuring. Surely he would not dress this way for her and like a down-at-heels footpad when actually plying the trade of highwayman.

Yet some doubts remained and after all it did not hurt to be cautious. "If you have come for the silver, you had better take care," she said, taunting him. "My uncle has set out a guard on the grounds."

"I know." He was clearly unconcerned. "He's sleeping under a tree near the orangery. Has it come to such a pass? Do you fear for your possessions? Yet you are here." She had walked out to meet him and he took her hands in his before she could prevent it. "Should I be gratified? This is a prize greater than silver, I think."

"I have come to tell you that you are not to come here again," she said with a calmness her heartbeat belied. "It is dangerous now that there has actually been a robbery, or rather an attempted one. My uncle fears alarm among our neighbors, but he is quietly taking steps to rout and capture the highwayman if he can."

"You seem to separate me from the act."

She felt a small tremor that she diagnosed as fear. "Should I not?"

He laughed in his throat. "But what else does a highwayman do?"

"Do you admit it then?" she asked, a bit breathless. She had not really expected this response.

"I admit to sometimes coveting what does not belong to me."

This remark echoed so exactly her own thoughts earlier in the evening that she shivered. She tried to draw her hands from his, but he held them fast. "I wonder that you have the courage to come here," she said.

"We aren't going to go through that nonsense about you screaming again, are we?" he asked wearily. "We both know you will not."

Catelyn knew he was right. "I meant what I said," she said fiercely, as much to convince herself as him. "I want you to leave and you must never come here again."

"Before I get what I came for?" he said insinuatingly, and drew her close to him.

"The silver?" she said mockingly. But her resistance

to him was only token; she expected this scene to be played out as the others had been, but somehow this time his embrace was different. Her pulse was quick—that was to be expected—but the melting feeling that his closeness usually brought to her was absent. She was not rigid in his arms, but she was not yielding.

He seemed to sense this and released her as suddenly as he had taken her in his arms. "What is it, Cat? Have you at last come to believe in me as Captain Black? Does that frighten you?" He laughed mirthlessly. "I would have thought that would have increased my appeal not lessened it."

She was inclined to agree with this; she did not know why she no longer wished for his embrace. Although the excuse he offered would do for him, she knew it was not the cause. "I admit the intrigue attracted me," she said, "but you have carried it further than I care to go. I would never succumb to a common thief, so you waste your time, sir, and had best go and not come back as I've said."

"I see," he said quietly, and, catching her by her wrist, pulled her against him again. "If I am a thief imitating a gentleman, it is quite another thing than if I were a gentleman imitating a thief." He entwined the fingers of his other hand in her hair and held her head firmly just inches from his own. "That spoils it for you, doesn't it? You like to think that I am really someone who leads you into the dance at insipid assemblies." He brought his lips suddenly against hers and she thought the kiss would be bruising but it was as gentle as the softest caress. "The play is over," he said into her ear, and let her go.

He turned and left her, quickly melting into the dark garden. Catelyn remained on the terrace for several minutes after he had gone. She knew that what he had said was true. It was over; she really would not see him again. Instead of feeling relieved as she had thought she would, she felt sad and suddenly very alone.

8

Never before in the whole of her life had the self-assured Catelyn Fitzsimon felt so completely *unsure* of herself. It was one thing to know that the masquerade of Captain Black was over and to resolve never to think of it again, it was quite another to do it. Somehow tied up in this was her confusion over the unexpected feelings she had had for Rhys that same night. But that with its firm basis in reality was the easier to deal with. It was the very insubstantialness of her involvement with the highwayman and the certainty that she should not have felt as she did about him that troubled her most.

True, she knew her feelings toward the man had undergone some undefined change, but she did not understand this any better than the other, and this was the worst of it. She felt the need to speak of it with someone, to help her to put her thoughts in order, but in whom could she confide with such intimacy?

Catelyn did miss her family and friends, the gaiety and glamour of the Season but not half so much as she had thought she would. The thing she did miss most, however, was having close friends to talk to. Her father was not the man to invite confidence from his daughter; her Aunt Philippa had seldom been sympa-

thetic to her problems; a great many of her friendships
were fairly shallow, based on going to the same places
at the same time with the same people for at least half
of every year. But there were one or two people to
whom Catelyn felt genuinely close, to whom she might
unburden herself if the need arose, and with these she
had corresponded faithfully since she had come to
Wales. Catelyn had described her initial meeting with
Black, but she had never mentioned the subsequent
meeting or the effect it had upon her, and she felt too
constrained to do so now.

Catelyn did not fear that her friends would mis-
understand her or judge her, but she doubted her own
ability to express her feelings properly on paper. What
she really wished for was someone who would understand her state of mind and help her turn her
confusion into order.

This was not a thing she could comfortably discuss
with a man, and among the women, her aunt,
Gwynne, and Bella were the only natural choices.
Catelyn felt loved and accepted by the Madoc family
despite the fact that she had been with them so short a
time; this was not why she hesitated to go to any one of
them. Her Aunt Bess was a kind woman, but Catelyn
doubted her ability to be objective about her meetings
with the highwayman.

Bella would undoubtedly be the most sympathetic
of the three. She would best understand the attraction
of Black; she would not blame Catelyn for so easily
succumbing to him. But Catelyn did not want rapt
attention and perfect commiseration from her
confidant, she wanted honest advice.

That left Gwynne, and though Catelyn felt least
close to her quiet cousin, she liked her very well and
valued her intelligence and understanding. Gwynne

would probably consider her meeting with a strange man unwise, and dangerous to her virtue and reputation, but she would not get caught up in the romance of it and her advice would doubtless be objective. Yet Catelyn found it difficult to broach the subject with Gwynne. Once or twice that next day she found herself alone with her cousin, and even made a small beginning, but each time she stayed her words at the last moment and went on to other topics.

She spent another semiwakeful night and knew that she would have to have advice at once if for no other reason than that at this rate, she was going to end up looking quite haggard.

Catelyn went down to breakfast quite early the following morning, ate quickly and sparingly, and deliberately sipped her chocolate so that she and Gwynne might quit the room at the same time.

As she came out of the breakfast room, Gwynne turned to her and said kindly, "Is something troubling you, Cat? I do not wish to pry, but I have felt since yesterday that you might wish to talk about some matter."

Catelyn was extremely grateful to have the difficulties of beginning glossed over, but she was also a bit taken aback by Gwynne's forthrightness. "Am I as obvious as that?" she asked with an uncertain laugh.

"Of course you are not," said Gwynne, linking her arm through Catelyn's. "But it seemed to me that you have been preoccupied of late and there are small smudges under your eyes that make me think you have not been sleeping well." The concern and sincerity of her tone could not be mistaken.

Catelyn's determination to tell Gwynne all strengthened. "I would like to talk to you if you would not mind," she said diffidently.

Gwynne smiled and led Catelyn into a small and seldom used saloon next to the book room. They seated themselves comfortably in chairs across from one another. Catelyn surreptitiously studied her cousin as they settled themselves; Gwynne looked so calm and serene, so much the embodiment of maidenly virtue that Catelyn almost lost heart. She did not believe that her behavior had been wanton, but she could not doubt for a moment that in her place, Gwynne would have resisted the highwayman's advances without the least difficulty, and she would certainly not be troubled by her feelings for him.

Because she could think of no satisfactory way to begin, Catelyn blurted out the story, doing a poor job of explaining the tumult of her own emotions and even admitting that she had allowed Captain Black to embrace and kiss her, a thing she had not intended to mention.

Gwynne listened blankly, neither commenting nor questioning. This disconcerted Catelyn and made her wonder why she had confided her problem at all. When she came to a somewhat stuttering end, silence fell between them and became awkward. Catelyn made no attempt to breach it, only wishing that this interview might be at an end. But when Gwynne finally spoke, Catelyn found it worse to bear than the silence.

"I do not know what to say to you, Cousin," Gwynne said. "I can scarcely credit what you have told me. How could you have behaved in such a way? I-I don't mean to ring a peal over you; it is scarcely my place to do so. But I am so shocked."

So was Catelyn. "Shocked? I know that what I have done was unwise . . ."

"Unwise?" Gwynne put her hands to her face in obvious distress. "Oh, Cousin, can you be so lost to all propriety? That you might meet any man in that clandestine fashion, but such a man! I cannot doubt that his ways were seducing and I know our sex can be vulnerable. If only you had come to me or Mama before it had gone so far. One must always be on guard to fight against our worst selves, and if one cannot control oneself, the constraints must come from one's friends."

Catelyn had always known that the secret meetings in the garden were not proper, but she felt that Gwynne's response was excessive. She felt humiliated in the face of Gwynne's obvious distaste and the guilt this forced upon her was turning to defensive anger. "I know I should not have gone out to the garden after the first time, Gwynne, but I was intrigued. I suppose I thought of it as an adventure." There was cool dignity in Catelyn's voice, not apology. "I was not, after all, seduced or ravished, and except for the first occasion when I encountered him at the gatehouse in all innocence, I never left the garden. It is not as if we met at some secret trysting place."

"That is just refining logic," Gwynne said severely. "Not even being raised in the looser society of London could make you unaware of what you have done."

"Perhaps it has," Catelyn retorted caustically. "For though I know it was not entirely the thing to do, I do not think it as dreadful as you seem to."

But Gwynne, whose distress was apparent by the way she twisted her handkerchief, heard no edge to Catelyn's voice. "I think society corrupts natural values. In spite of the reason your papa sent you to us, I cannot think that you are lost to decency, Catelyn.

Though I have seen you many times in company, I have never witnessed any conduct in you that was not pleasing, and I think in your heart you are a good woman."

Gwynne rose and walked slowly around to the back of her chair, showing as much discomposure as Catelyn had ever witnessed in her. It was on the tip of Catelyn's tongue to thank her tartly for her "approbation" but she saw that her cousin was not self-righteous but sincere and that Gwynne was finding this as distressful as she herself was.

"I am sure that it is youth and high spirits which have made you behave so," Gwynne said, resuming her speech. "No doubt you are unconscious of the risk to your reputation, to say nothing to your person. As you say, he did you no physical harm, but he might have and he still may intend to if you continue in this course. I know you wished this to be kept in confidence," Gwynne added unhappily, "but I feel I must tell Mama what you have told me."

Catelyn was astonished at these words. "Gwynne! I beg you will not. I came to you for advice because I did not wish to discuss this with my aunt."

"I know. But I do not feel qualified to advise you on such a delicate matter and I must assure myself that you will not again do such a thing. Mama will take measures to make it impossible. You told me yourself that you had already resolved never to meet him again but could not resist the temptation." She met Catelyn's eyes for the first time in many minutes. "I am sorry, Cat, but truly, I must do this."

Catelyn did not respond. There was no point in doing so. She knew Gwynne would never shrink from anything she perceived as her duty, however unpleasant. Catelyn was hurt by her cousin's response and quite angry, but as much at herself for misreading Gwynne's seeming sympathy as at her cousin's betrayal.

After a moment or two of uncomfortable silence, Gwynne left, and Catelyn did nothing to stop her.

As Rhys came down the hall he saw Gwynne leave the saloon. But she turned in the opposite direction and proceeded down the hall without noticing his presence. It was obvious to him that she was in some distress, but he did not feel that he should go after her, so he continued on and entered the book room.

A curious sight greeted him. Hu was closing a door with great care and stealth. He heard Rhys enter and put a finger to his lips. He moved away from the door and did not speak until he was nearly in the middle of the room. Rhys made himself comfortable in one of the leather chairs, waiting to have the mystery unraveled.

Hu's smile was more of a smirk. "My Cousin Edward Mantery had more of an escape than he knew."

"Who is Edward Mantery?"

"My Aunt Mantery's son," Hu replied cryptically, but added for clarity, "the poor devil that thought to take Catelyn to the altar."

Rhys raised his brows at this, but otherwise his expression was unreadable. "I thought you thought him a fool for letting such 'a pretty piece' with such a comfortable dowry to sweeten the pot slip through his fingers?"

"Cat is a diamond of the first water," Hu conceded, "and fifty thousand with more to come when Fitzsimon kicks off is a cream pot of the first order, but unless a man's pockets are to let, it seems to me that other comforts ought to be a consideration too."

"Oh, undoubtedly," Rhys said at his blandest, and went over to the concealed cabinet that held Madeira and other light refreshment for visitors. "And you think that Catelyn would not make a comfortable wife?"

"Would you want a wife who was forever running about the countryside with all manner of strange men?"

"I doubt I would want a wife who ran anywhere with any other man."

"Exactly." Hu accepted the glass of Madeira that Rhys handed to him.

When Hu made no further attempt to explain his words, Rhys prompted him. "Is that what Catelyn does?"

"I told you how she ran off with some fellow to Scotland, jilting Mantery. The only reason it wasn't a total disgrace was because my Uncle Fitzsimon caught up with them before the first night was spent on the road."

From the easy way that Rhys regarded him, Hu had no notion of the intensity of his interest or of his displeasure with Hu's loose words. "An ill-advised attempt to escape an unhappy engagement, I believe you told me," Rhys said levelly. "Is that sufficient for you to make such a damning statement?"

Hu shrugged. "I make it only to you, dear boy. I can tell you, though, if word of her latest scrape gets out, she'd be lucky to have the sweep offer for her."

If Rhys had had any lingering doubts that it was Hu's indiscretion that had made Catelyn's meeting with him as Captain Black the talk of the neighborhood, it was erased. Hu's careless gossip about her set up his back, but he could not resist wanting to know what Hu would say of her now. "What scrape?" he asked brusquely.

"That's what I was about when you came in," Hu said, lowering his voice conspiratorially. "The door into the saloon next to us was ajar and I heard Catelyn and Gwynne in there talking. The short of it is Cat's been meeting with that fellow calling himself Captain Black, not just that first time at the gatehouse, which was accident, but since then and right here at the house. Fellow's been making love to her too," he added with apparent relish, "and more, she's been letting him."

Rhys felt his fist clench involuntarily and Hu probably never knew how close he was to having his cork drawn at that moment. Unperturbed and unsuspecting, Hu went on blithely, "Doesn't know now if she's on her head or her heels about the thing so she asked Gwynne her advice. Silly gudgeon thing to do. *I* could have told her that it was bird-witted to expect Gwynne to understand a thing like that. Gwynne is the best of good sisters, but she's proper to a fault, never understands that one has to kick up one's heels every once in a while. But I suppose I should not be saying that to you. It is not precisely a bad quality in a wife, but not one I much care for. Still, when *you* have your fun, you'd best be discreet."

The reference to a distant future when he would make Gwynne his wife annoyed Rhys. Only his good breeding kept him from pointing out that he had never offered for Gwynne, or so much as hinted to her or the Madocs that he would one day do so. His conduct toward her had always been that of a brother toward a sister and that was what they were to each other. For some time of late he had known that he would *never* choose Gwynne for his wife and he disliked the hints of its likelihood.

But more to the purpose now was the discussion at hand. "I hope then that your wife is more understanding," Rhys said acerbically, "for certainly discretion is not your strong suit. Whether Gwynne was sympathetic to Catelyn or not, it was doubtless meant to be a confidence and you had no right to listen and even less right to pass the story on to me."

Hu looked surprised and even hurt. It was obvious from his expression that he saw no wrong in what he had done. "I said before, it's only to you that I say it."

"It was not meant for either of us to hear. I can only hope that you do not mean to make the neighborhood a present of the information as you did the first time she met Black."

"That's not fair, Rhys," Hu said, defensive, but no more than casually so. "Until of late when she took it in her mind to dislike it, I never heard that she wanted it kept quiet. Made her quite a hit at the Cardiff Assembly and she was fussed over for a fortnight after it. Didn't hear her complain about that."

Rhys regarded him for a long moment. Hu clearly saw no blame in what he had done and Rhys knew from long experience that it was unlikely that pointing it out to him even in terms a child would understand would have any great effect. Remaining and feeding his own anger was equally pointless. He lifted himself out of the chair slowly, saying, "Actually, I came by to see your father. The fence on the northern border of Llanbryth where our properties meet is down again."

Rhys walked to the door, but there he turned again toward Hu, who was still seated sipping at his Madeira. "Whatever the case was last time, Hu, you came by this information on Catelyn unfairly and it would be dishonorable for you to repeat it. To anyone."

Hu sighed with patent exasperation. "Sometimes I think I am surrounded by a damned lot of sanctimonious prigs. I never thought it of you before, Rhys, but I think running Llanbryth yourself like a damned steward has had a lowering effect on your character. Marry Gwynne as soon as may be; she'll make you the perfect wife. You can spend your evenings pinching pennies and clucking over the laxities of your family and friends. Matter of fact," he added after the briefest of pauses while he poured more of the wine, "you ought to make the acquaintance of Bella's papa next time you are in Cardiff. He's an expert at doing both."

Rhys stood with his hand on the door, listening to this speech. He did not take offense at it; instead a faint smile touched his lips. "The cream pot turning sour, Hu? Didn't you look to your comfort when you married Bella?"

"I'm dashed fond of Bella," Hu said, his brows snapping together. "I don't need her father's money; I'll have Madoc one day. It isn't a crime to want the best things one can have if it's possible, is it?"

"No. It's not even a crime to want the best of everything even if it isn't possible," Rhys said mildly. "Do you know where I may find Sir Thomas?"

Hu waved an impatient hand. "In the stables, perhaps," he said, and then gave his attention to draining his glass, his deliberate rudeness to Rhys the only overt sign that some of what his friend had said to him had discomfited him.

9

Catelyn did not know whether she was more angry or hurt by Gwynne's unexpected reaction to the confidence she had shared with her. She did not doubt for a minute that Gwynne had been serious when she said that she would go to Lady Madoc, and so Catelyn went up to her room to anxiously await the expected summons from her aunt.

The summons did come finally and the interview proved to be excessively unpleasant. Lady Madoc did not rant as Catelyn's father did, she did not weep and call her ungrateful as was the custom of Cateyln's Aunt Philippa. She simply asked Catelyn to confirm the story told to her by Gwynne, and when Catelyn had done so, Lady Madoc had looked disappointed and most unhappy. This upset Catelyn far more than ranting or weeping could have done.

"I'm sure I don't know what I should do," Lady Madoc said in a tone that made it clear that she wished she would be visited by a sudden revelation of her clear duty. "I am sure that you meant no harm in what you have done, that it was most innocent. Gwynne said you spoke of it as an adventure."

"I suppose that was foolish of me," Catelyn admitted, sitting across from her aunt in the latter's dressing room. "I did not think very much of the impropriety of what I was doing at the time, but I can see now that it might be construed as something far different from what it was."

"Gwynne also said that you . . . that this man . . . that he . . . well, made advances," Lady Madoc finished uncomfortably.

"He kissed me," Catelyn said flatly. "That I know I should not have allowed. I have no excuse."

Lady Madoc rose nervously from her chair. "The worst of it is I know I should tell your papa. But if you will forgive me for speaking so of your father, Richard was never an easy man to deal with, at least not as a brother. So I would as lief not to do so, though I am sure Sir Thomas will say I should."

"Must you tell Sir Thomas?"

"I don't know," Lady Madoc said. She truly did not want to go to her brother or husband with this. She understood what had led Catelyn to this and did not really question Catelyn's virtue, but if there should be any difficulties in the future and it came out that she had known and had kept the information to herself, there would doubtless be the devil to pay.

Sighing forcefully, she said at last, "Perhaps if you give me your solemn promise never to meet with this man again and if you so much as see him in the garden or near the house to at once raise an alarm, then we might just consider this an unhappy incident. It is not as if anyone knows of it and your reputation is in danger. Thank God for that. Not even your papa would be able to gloss over such a scandal. A highwayman! Why we might all have been murdered in our beds!"

"I do give you my word, Aunt Bess, that I shall never again meet with Captain Black or even seek to do so." As she knew he would not come to her again it was an easy enough promise to make. She did not mention the second part of the promise that her aunt wished, for if she ever did see him again, she had no intention of calling the house down on him. "But I do not think," she could not help adding, "that there was ever much chance that any one of us would come to any harm from this man. He called himself Captain Black, but I don't believe he was really a highwayman."

Lady Madoc looked surprised. "How can you say so after what you witnessed the other day coming from Taff Wyd? This man has attacked a carriage and it may even have been he who robbed Mrs. Sommers's friend. He is dangerous and unscrupulous."

Catelyn was no longer sure what she believed, but she did not want to think that Captain Black was the real highwayman. "I am certain it was mere coincidence," she said in a tone she hoped was convincing.

"Oh, my dear, I cannot be so sanguine." Lady Madoc did not precisely wring her hands, but she looked as if she would have liked to. "But if you do promise . . ." She let her voice trail of suggestively. She wanted the interview to be over every bit as much as her niece wished it. Fortunately, she was saved by the unheralded entrance of her daughter-in-law.

"I have been looking for you this age, Cat," Bella said without apologizing for her intrusion or even being aware that it was one. "Laurie has been here this quarter hour to take us to visit with the Tremaines and he is chafing to have his horses standing all this time. Goodness, you are not even dressed!" she added with some surprise.

Catelyn was tempted to cry off at once, but it

occurred to her that getting away from Madoc Hall for a few hours would be preferable to spending the day with the cousin she had shocked or the aunt she had disappointed—or alone in her room like a bad child being punished. Instead, she asked and received prompt permission from her aunt to be excused from their interview and she quickly returned to her room to change.

But by the time her maid answered her summons, Catelyn had changed her mind again and sent word to Bella to go on without her. Feeling dispirited by the events of the morning, she decided that a penitent day would suit her mood after all. But no quiet activity could contain her swift and troubled thoughts and it was a clear sign of her inner turmoil that once again she mistook her own mind.

This time she sought to combine solitude and activity and she changed into a dark blue velvet riding habit. She did not have a servant send a message to the stables to have a horse brought around for her, as was the usual custom for the ladies of the house, but went directly to the stables herself—quietly and unobserved, she hoped.

Catelyn went down the service stairs, encountered no one, and let herself out of the house through the garden. It was in full spring bloom, but she was immune to its beauty. Gardens, in particular this garden, would never be a place of serenity to her again. She walked along the gravel paths, cutting through the kitchen garden and across a small stretch of green without looking either to the right or left of her.

Catelyn intended to insist on riding the most spirited hack in her uncle's stable. She had had the finest riding masters and was an accomplished horsewoman. She had no fear of a difficult mount and wanted a challenging exercise. She knew that she would have to deal with all the things that had occurred in her life since she had first made that innocent visit to the gatehouse, but just now she did not want to think of Captain Black, Gwynne, Rhys, or even her own values.

She astonished the groom, first because he was not used to the ladies of the house coming to the stables to collect their mounts, and second, because she demanded a horse that none but Sir Thomas or Hu Madoc had ever ridden. He felt obliged to steer her toward a quieter ride, but she was adamant.

Catelyn went into the tack room to wait. It was a small room, its walls entirely lined with saddles, bridles, and harnessing on pegs. It smelled richly of leather, saddle soap, and horse. There was a small, very dirty window that faced onto a rear paddock where a blacksmith was shoeing one of the carriage horses. For want of a better occupation, Catelyn watched him until she heard someone entering the room and turned.

It was not the groom to tell her her horse was ready, but Rhys. "Oh, it's you," she said in such unwelcoming accents that he blinked.

"Yes," he said evenly, "it's me. Do you know you've given Gus, the second groom, something of a moral dilemma? On the one hand, he is trained to do as he is told, but on the other, he fears that if you can't handle Strider and break your neck, he will have to live with the blame for it."

For the first time that day a faint smile appeared on Catelyn's features. "I can handle Strider. My riding instructor was once horsemaster at Astley's Circus. He taught me to handle just about anything."

"You would make Gus a good deal easier if you allowed a groom to go out with you," Rhys persisted. "At a reasonable distance, if you prefer."

Catelyn was in no humor to suffer his officiousness. "I do not mean to leave the estate," she said.

"I was thinking of your safety," he said mildly.

"Thank you," she said with a softening of her tone. "But I assure you I do not exaggerate my abilities." She turned and again looked out the window. The smallness of the room perforce brought him near to her. As it had been on the terrace that night, at once she was conscious of his maleness and this was disconcerting. She had no wish to further complicate her already complicated life by encouraging him. She hoped that he would take her hint and leave her, but he did not.

"I seem to have a knack for offending you," he said quietly, but with some other, odd inflection in his voice that made her turn to him again. "I am not sure what I have done this time, but I was not questioning your behavior or ability. One doesn't have to ride out very far to encounter dangers that have nothing to do with either of those things."

As was so often the case, she could not tell from his expression or tone if there was more to his words than what appeared on the surface, but she was reasonably certain that this was another oblique reference to Captain Black, or rather it suited her to think that. It made her angry with him. "Sometimes dangers can be found in one's own garden," she said icily.

"Sometimes nearer than that."

There was no doubt about his tone now; it was distinctly dry and, she thought, somehow assured. It made her catch her breath. "She told you!" Instantly she thought that Gwynne had betrayed her yet again. Tears of hurt and anger stung her eyes.

He seemed mildly astonished. "Who told me what?"

"You needn't bother to try to save face for her," Catelyn said bitingly. "If Gwynne does not approve of the confidence entrusted in her, it is clear that she feels no compunction to honor it."

Rhys's own feelings for the woman who stood before him, anger making her eyes flash and her cheeks tint with color, were very far from untroubled. Catelyn was not the only one who felt the attraction, not the only one who feared its complications. It was worse for him, for though he had the advantage of knowing the truth about Captain Black, he felt it as a disadvantage. Unlike Catelyn he understood his feelings fairly well, but he feared to put them to the test.

When he was disguised as Captain Black, she was intrigued, attracted, excited. Whenever he met her as himself, she was indifferent, annoyed, contemptuous. He had no idea at all how to reconcile the extremes. But at all costs he had no wish to hurt her, and her distress was clear now. He knew it was not the time to dissemble further but neither was it the time for revelation.

"You are mistaken," he said firmly. "Gwynne told me nothing about you. I give you my word on that as a gentleman."

She faced him fully. She could not doubt what he said as the truth. "But you know that I have met Captain Black again and in the garden?" she said tentatively, beginning to fear that her sensitivity to the subject had caused her to give herself away.

By this point, Rhys was heartily wishing himself elsewhere. There were already too many lies between them, so many that he feared they might be past explaining. He was as honest with her as he dared to be at this point. "Your confidences to Gwynne were overheard."

"By you?" She looked her complete puzzlement, but after a moment her features cleared. "Hu. Damn him!" She slashed angrily at the nearest saddle with her crop and turned away again, this time because the tears that stung at her eyes began to overspill. All of a sudden she knew that she was angry because of all men on earth, this was the one she least wished to think ill of her.

"I am sorry," he said gently. "I truly did not mean to tease you in such a way over such a thing. I don't know why I said such a thing. I suppose I thought you would not understand me."

"Oh, I understand," she said in watery accents. "I understand what you think. Don't bother to deny it. The opinion you admitted to having of me when we first met is doubtless confirmed."

"I thought we agreed that our first impressions of each other were completely wrong."

"And our last impressions?" she said scathingly. She took a sustaining breath and successfully steadied the part of her that wanted to dissolve completely into tears of hurt and self-pity. "If you will excuse me, sir," she said with cool dignity, "I think that after all, I shall not ride." She gave him no opportunity to reply but swept past him.

When Catelyn reached the house, she thought for certain that she would at last give in to her tears, but she did not. She did not really think what she would do next, she simply did it.

Feeling oddly buoyant, she opened the small portable writing desk with which she always traveled, and mending her pen, she wrote at once to her father.

Her dutiful weekly letters to her father and Aunt Philippa had never once hinted at her meeting with Captain Black or that there was anything at all to disturb the absolute serenity of her visit. Doubtless her father was by now preparing for his usual remove to Brighton. He had made it clear to her that her disgrace was to extend beyond this time and that the soonest she could look to an end to her exile was the end of July when he journeyed from Brighton to Kent to spend his customary fortnight at his principal seat before beginning a round of visits to the houses of his friends.

Catelyn had no idea what he would make of her penitential letter. It was very like her to admit she was wrong, but not at all in her usual style to plead her cause in a begging way. She wrote slowly, carefully choosing her words so as not to make it seem as if the Madocs had made her unhappy or uncomfortable. She would have enjoyed making a few animadverisions on the character of Hu, but she restrained herself and tried her best to make it seem as if only homesickness was the source of her request to return to his household.

There was the possibility that her father was still angry with her and would refuse to allow her to return to him. In that case, there was nothing for it. But the truth was, her father was not a man to carry his anger. His reaction to her behavior had been strong, but it was doubtful that he even now thought of the near scandal she had caused. If she wished to be forgiven, he would probably forgive, at least as soon as it was convenient for him to do so.

When she finished her letter, Catelyn read it over carefully. She dusted it with sand and sealed it with a monogrammed wafer. She then took it downstairs and placed it with the rest of the letters that the butler would soon take into the village for posting. She then returned to her room, satisfied with this positive action and determined not to question what she had done.

10

Her father was an indifferent correspondent, so Catelyn knew she would have to wait for his reply. She composed herself as best she could for the possibility of her meetings with Captain Black becoming known to the neighborhood, but apparently Hu had the sense this time to hold his tongue. It made her breathe easier, but she did not regret having written to her father.

She had come to love Madoc and the surrounding countryside. Just as she had once regarded life in the country as insipid, now she thought the endless social life in town vapid. But though she might wish to remain at Madoc, she knew it was not right for her to do so and not just because of Captain Black.

She had kept her word to her aunt. She had not once looked or listened for the highwayman since that day; she actively shunned the garden the moment it turned twilight. But she knew she was just paying lip service to the promise she had made; Captain Black would not again return to her.

Her wayward thoughts were not so easily tamed. A sense of loss troubled her most. She called herself a fool a thousand times but could not help longing for the excitement of Captain Black. It was clear to her that the romance and not the reality of him had attracted her, but meeting him in that clandestine way and courting the danger of his presence had been a delicious, almost narcotic thrill.

And this was what she mourned for! Catelyn was almost able to step outside of herself and wonder at the absurd creature she had become. As if this were not enough, the only other man to figure in her thoughts was Rhys.

In some ways this surprised her the more. She could understand the forbidden lure of the highwayman, but despite what Rhys had said, she was not even sure that Rhys liked her, and certainly he was not at all the sort of man to whom she was usually attracted. He did not attempt to pay her pretty, empty compliments, nor did he seem to have the least interest in her fortune or social standing in the world. He did not live for sporting pursuits as did Laurie; he had no apparent interest in the most fashionable width of lapels as did her Cousin Edward. He seldom made pointless small talk and his time and energies were generally directed toward his responsibilities rather than his pleasures.

Less than two months ago she had thought him dull; now she was forced to admit that he interested her more than any man she knew, with the possible exception of Captain Black, and he was not of the real world as was Rhys. She could only wonder what had wrought this change in her feelings toward him. She supposed it might be the contrast, laid out, as it were, in sharp perspective, between Rhys and Laurence.

Laurence was a very likable young man, and exactly the type she had supposed to be most to her liking. But seen beside his brother, Laurie's character appeared rather ordinary and even shallow. He was just one more young man bent on using his looks and wits to impress a world that was no longer impressionable.

These thoughts came to her piecemeal over the next few days, which were not sufficiently filled to prevent her giving time to them, and they had melded into this whole by the Friday of the week she had written to her father.

The moon was again at the full and the Madocs were to travel nearly to Rhondda to the ball being given in honor of the betrothal of Lady Tremaine's son. It was the first major evening entertainment since the Cardiff Assembly and Catelyn was looking forward to it. She fully intended to flirt with every young man who caught her fancy, hoping in this way to remove from her mind the two men she did not wish to think of.

Catelyn felt more comfortable about going in to company by this time, now that she was reasonably certain of Hu's discretion. A few favored guests including the Madocs and the Trefors had been invited to dinner as well, and as Catelyn was not seated near Rhys, she enjoyed the meal very much. Not even the specter of Captain Black was introduced into the conversation to cut up her peace, though of course there was some talk of her and Laurie's rescue of Lord Tremaine's future daughter-in-law from the would-be highwayman. But no one chose to make the connection between this and Catelyn's known meeting with Captain Black.

A young man named Kearney, whom Catelyn had not met before, was seated next to her and his manner and expression from the moment of introduction left no doubt in the minds of all observers that he was utterly enchanted. Mr. Kearney was the first gentleman to plead for a dance and he showed every evidence that he meant to cleave to Catelyn's side for the whole of the evening if she would allow it. He was a pleasant enough young man, though his conversation was not fluid, but she did not wish for his exclusive company. To shake him proved impossible. During her dances with other young men, he watched her in a tiresome, brooding manner. At the end of each set he was waiting to claim her again for as long as he could.

After half an evening of this, Catelyn was becoming quite exasperated and only the wish not to wound him prevented her from sharp words. Quite unconsciously, her eyes appealed to Rhys, and though she was reasonably sure he understood, his only response was an amused smile cast her way before he returned to a conversation with his hostess. Laurie, who was nearly beside him, saw her glance too and was more gallant. At once he extricated himself from Mrs. Sommers, with whom he had been speaking, and came over to Catelyn and Mr. Kearney.

"Mrs. Sommers is most anxious to form a table for whist, Cat," he said to her without preamble as he approached. "Will you join us to make a fourth? I know Kearney will excuse you."

Like Laurie, Catelyn found whist a tedious game, but she played it well enough and any excuse that would force Mr. Kearney to turn his attention elsewhere was welcome. "I should enjoy it above all things," she said with bright untruth. Murmuring a brief excuse to the ubiquitous young man, she allowed Laurie to take her arm and lead her to Mrs. Sommers, her daughter, and Mr. Howell.

Mr. Kearney was not so easily routed. He boldly followed Catelyn and Laurie and did not hesitate to state that he wished he might make one of their number, though it was obvious that he was a fifth and unnecessary. Mr. Howell, who had been bullied into joining them by Mrs. Sommers, was quick to cry off.

Seeing the dark look this produced on the countenance of Mrs. Sommers and thinking that it might be an escape for her as well, Catelyn said quickly, "No, I would not hear of it, Mr. Howell. In fact, I only said I wished to play to make your fourth. If Mr. Kearney wishes to play, then I would be most glad to give him my place." This suited no one and all protested, Mr. Kearney the most loudly, but after his earnest desire to make one of their number, he could not gracefully extricate himself and Catelyn was quick to make her escape.

The set for the next dance was already forming and Catelyn did not have a partner, but she did not mind. In fact, she half feared that Kearney would escape her machinations after all and so she decided to leave the ballroom.

The ballroom was on the second floor in the center wing of the house and a room had been set aside on the floor below for the ladies to rest between dances and refresh their appearance. Catelyn went down to this room, but unhappily it was already occupied by Miss Jorwarth, with one of her usual satellites in attendance.

"It is a shocking squeeze, is it not?" said Miss Jorwarth to Catelyn as soon as she came in.

The term "squeeze," which was often applied to entertainments by hostesses who thought the success of their parties was directly proportional to the number of people they could cram into their rooms at one time, scarcely applied in the present instance; the comment was pure affectation. "I am sure Lady Tremaine is pleased with the number of people who were able to come tonight," Catelyn said noncommittally. A number of mirrors had been hung about the room and Catelyn went over to one of them to pat an already perfect curl. Her excuse for being there taken care of, she prepared to leave, for she had no taste for the company.

Catelyn heard murmurs behind her and then, sounding reluctant, the other young woman, who was unknown to Catelyn, said, "Your journey here tonight was uneventful, Miss Fitzsimon?'"

Catelyn stiffened; given the fact that the comment was doubtless prompted by Miss Jorwarth, she could guess its import. "Quite," she said in a quelling voice.

"We though you might perhaps have been accosted on the way by a highwayman," Miss Jorwarth said with false sweetness. "One never knows when one will appear in these parts."

Catelyn did not deign to answer this, but left the room without apparent haste or in any other way showing the extent of her annoyance. When she was at last in Brighton or Kent or wherever with her father, it was her earnest desire never to so much as hear the word "highwayman" or the name "Captain Black" again.

The music floating down from above made it clear the dancing had begun again and the corridor leading to the stairs and the ballroom was now completely empty. Other than the distant strains of the music, there was no sound at all where she was, and she had the eerie sensation of being completely alone, though there were more than a hundred people in the house. Knowing that she could feel this way with so many near to her gave her an odd sense of peace and she did not rush up the stairs to join the company as she had intended, but remained beside the foot of the stairs, content to listen to the music, a peace in itself after being plagued by Mr. Kearney and Miss Jorwarth.

Catelyn stayed there for some time until approaching voices told her that the two young women were coming her way. She sighed and supposed she had best return to the ballroom, for she had no wish to encounter them again, but before she could move to do so, she heard unmistakably masculine footsteps descending the stairs. She could not look up to see who it was without coming around the stairs enough to give herself away. She had a sudden horrific vision of finding herself trapped between Mr. Kearney and Miss Jorwarth. The corridor leading into the west wing was almost opposite from her and, impulsively, she scurried into it, hoping to escape notice.

It was in darkness, with only the light from the center hall spreading a dull glow a short way into the wing, and she walked into the deep shadows to a window overlooking the grounds. As she reached it she heard a greeting exchanged in the main hall, though she could not recognize the male voice from that distance. The footsteps then resumed going away from her and she could only suppose she was unobserved.

The moonlight was so bright that once her eyes adjusted to the greater darkness, the corridor no longer seemed dark at all. She looked out the window onto the smooth, shaved lawn. The inevitable, unbidden thought of that first night that she had wandered to the gatehouse popped into her head, and this made her smile wryly. She might say to herself that Miss Jorwarth's spiteful comment had put Black back into her mind, but she knew the thought needed no such assistance.

Since the hall was carpeted and she was absorbed in her thoughts, Catelyn heard no sound of approach; the first notion she had that she was not alone was when he spoke her name. That soft, deliberately throaty tone was unmistakable. After a moment of doubting her ears, her heart began to beat in her breast in a hard way and a strange lethargy seemed to come over her limbs. She turned, quite slowly, and if she had doubted her ears, she now did not believe her eyes. "You," she gasped.

There was no doubting his identity in the moonlight; she knew Rhys too well. His expression was unreadable, but his smile was faintly mocking.

"Did you think you wouldn't see me again, Cat?" he asked quietly.

Catelyn was so stunned to think that this man of all men was Captain Black that she was momentarily bereft of speech.

"No caustic comment? No quick rejoinder?" he asked, speaking now in his normal tone. "It is that I am the last choice to masquerade as a highwayman, is it not?"

"Yes," she said baldly, causing him to laugh self-mockingly. Catelyn was not precisely disappointed to discover the truth, but she was not pleased. Given her recent thoughts of the merging of the two men who so attracted her into one man should have settled much of her confusion, but if anything, it made it worse.

Out of her chaotic emotions, one feeling emerged, a sense of betrayal, a burgeoning notion that he had somehow used her for his own purposes. "Why would you do this?" she demanded.

"I too have a fancy for night air," he said in a flip way.

"And for romantic intrigue?"

"Yes, so it would seem."

"I suppose even farmers must have their amusements." She heard him catch his breath at this and knew she had hit the mark. She couldn't say why she was reacting in this way, but she was conscious of a feeling of vulnerability and supposed it must be the cause. "I thought better of you," she added in a less offensive tone.

"You were not so critical of my 'amusements' when I held you in my arms on the terrace," he was stung into replying. It was her turn to draw in her breath sharply and he said at once, "I beg your pardon, Cat. I should not have said that."

"Why not?" she said waspishly. "It is stupid to pretend that we do not know what has occurred between us, though you had the cruel advantage of knowing it when I did not."

"I didn't mean for it to be this way. It began by accident and I never really meant it to go on, but when it did . . . I knew I would have to tell you. I nearly did so that night I followed you to the Gold Saloon."

"So stricken was your conscience," she said in dulcet accents, "that you went home, cut holes in your scarf, and came back here to throw gravel at my window."

"Are you upset because I did this," he asked quietly, "or because you came to me?"

"Both," she said with flat honesty. "How could you use me in such a way and then offer me friendship? Did you enjoy laughing in your sleeve when you

warned me of the dangers of meeting with a highwayman? Did you feel smug when I insisted that I could
not be tempted by his lures?"

"No, it was never that way."

"It wasn't? Then explain it to me, Rhys, I don't at
all understand."

"I don't understand myself," he said, looking away
from her again to the window. "At least, I didn't until
very recently. It did begin in accident when you found
me at the gatehouse—and not for the reason you
would suppose. I had no thought of it going on, but I
found I had to see you again in that way."

"Had to?"

"Yes." He faced her again. "Why did *you* come
down to the garden again? Did you think an attraction
that strong would not be mutual?"

"You assume . . ."

"I don't think I do," he said softly, and, without
touching her any other way, bent his head and kissed
her very gently.

It happened so quickly that Catelyn had no time for
thought, and though she knew he was no longer a
mysterious highwayman and the lure of his forbidden-
ness was gone, her response was as strong as ever it was
in the garden. But she would have hidden this from
him if she could and she turned her shoulder to him.

"If you felt this way about me," she said in a voice
that she had to consciously control, "why could you
not approach me in the normal way? Why would you
do this thing to make me seem foolish and wicked even
to myself."

"Oh, Lord, I never meant that." He put out a hand
as if to touch her but knew it would be rejected and
stayed the gesture. "You know how poorly we began,"

he said dryly. "I don't think advances from me would have found any sure welcome."

"I am surprised you would wish to make any toward me." She turned back to him.

"It surprised me too," he said with a wry smile. "Cat, I . . ."

"And then of course there is Gwynne and the Madocs to think of," she said, not letting him finish. "It would have been a trifle awkward to press your suit to me under the noses of your betrothed and her family."

"Gwynne and I are not betrothed."

"Not formally, but everyone knows how it is between you. Did you suppose I would not hear of it?"

"*Everyone* does not know how it is between Gwynne and me," he said tartly. "*Everyone* assumes and they assume incorrectly."

"Oh, lovely!" she said brightly. "You make love surreptitiously to me, amuse yourself with the private knowledge of it, and now you seek to dishonor the woman you have pledged yourself to. What a delightful example of a gentleman you are, to be certain." She knew that he was a man to whom honor would matter and that her words could only cut him. Catelyn was not a woman to lightly trample the feelings of another, especially when that other was someone for whom she cared. But it was because she did care for this man and because he had the power to wound her that she wished to strike back at him.

But he did not respond in kind. "I didn't admit to masquerading as Black for it to come between us. I don't wish for things to be this way."

"They can be no other way," she said coldly, and turned and left him. She heard him come after her and quickened her steps. Almost as soon as she entered the main hall, she saw Mr. Kearney coming down the stairs with her Aunt Bess in tow.

"Where have you been, Catelyn?" the older woman said almost peevishly. "Mr. Kearney was most concerned when he found you had left the ballroom and would have me search for you in case you were taken ill." She cast a baleful look at that young man and then looked to her niece again for an explanation.

What humor Catelyn had had in dealing with the annoying man had since vanished. Her cheeks felt warm and she supposed her color was high. For all she knew, Rhys would come out of the west wing at any moment and what her aunt would think of that she could only guess. But she was in no humor to concoct lengthy explanations and she certainly owed none to Mr. Kearney, whose attentions she had never sought in the first place.

"I found the ballroom warm and wished to rest for a few minutes," she said frostily. "I was unaware that I needed first to inform Mr. Kearney of my intentions."

Mr. Kearney flushed at these words and Lady Madoc looked taken aback by her niece's unaccustomed rudeness. The young man hastily mumbled an excuse and finally took himself in search of more congenial company. Catelyn was glad enough to follow her aunt back to the ballroom now that she was rid of him.

"Are you feeling well, Cat?" Lady Madoc asked as they mounted the stairs.

"I am only a bit warm, Aunt," she responded, and Lady Madoc did not pursue the matter.

Seeing Rhys return to the ballroom, Catelyn chose to ignore him; she did not stand up with him for the whole of the evening or even exchange another word with him before the Madoc party left, which was in the early hours of the morning not long before the moon had set.

11

The confusion that Rhys had caused in Catelyn's mind and heart was not greater than that which he had engendered in his own. He had fallen into the role of Captain Black by accident and he had kept it up to tease the arrogant Miss Fitzsimon, to whom he had been unadmittedly attracted since their first meeting. But he knew the truth of his feelings for her now, and as it was with Catelyn, the truth only made him more confused.

It was early in the morning following the Tremaine Ball and although Rhys was by custom an early riser, he had been bidden from his bed betimes by an urgent message from Cardiff. His uncle Lord Trefor's illness had again taken a bad turn and his physician had sent word that he did not expect the old man to live through another day. For reasons of propriety, as he was his uncle's heir, if not for affection, it behooved Rhys to go to Cardiff at once. But he felt no moral obligation to be at the bedside of his reclusive relative who in any case probably did not wish to have him there. Rhys had always honored his uncle's wish to be left alone.

His impulse, in fact, was to send a message that he could not leave Llanbryth but would of course come at once to Cardiff to see to all the arrangements should his uncle expire. However, he was too well bred to shrink from what was expected of him, and in the end he decided that it was no bad thing to absent himself from the neighborhood for a time.

He didn't know that time and distance would help to dissolve the obstacles to his happiness, but at the least they would give his thoughts the perspective he believed he needed. So the message he did send to Cardiff was that he would see to one or two pressing matters of estate business and then come at once. Those matters were now cleared and he waited only for his brother to come down to breakfast. When Laurie did so, Rhys would apprise him of their uncle's state and ask if Laurie wished to accompany him.

He chose to wait in his study, tallying an account of the production of the home farm. But very little of his mind was on his work; most of it was on the events of the previous night.

Though he had assured Catelyn of the nobility of his motives, in the light of day, he wondered at them himself. Whatever these had been, he had known the night that he had followed her into the Gold Saloon at Madoc Hall that it was no longer just a game to him, that he was in deadly earnest. He had not seized that moment but had chosen instead to continue with the disguise for one last time. He could only wonder now if this folly had not cost him all. He was hurt by Catelyn's words but understood how she must feel used by him. It was truth when he told her that he had not meant it in that way, but it was not astonishing that she could not believe him.

Rhys ran his fingers down yet another column of figures that he did not see. Last night's interview had left him dispirited and discouraged. It was more than her anger and disbelief over his motives. He felt he was no fit match for Catelyn Fitzsimon of London and Kent and God knew where else! If his uncle should die, his own position would be improved, but he would still be no great prize on the Marriage Mart. Catelyn, with her beauty, fortune and connections, could look as high as she pleased and he wondered at this arrogant supposition that she would wish to marry him.

There was yet another thing to cut up his peace. It was true that he did not consider himself betrothed or in any way bound in promise to Gwynne, but it was also true, as Catelyn had said, that everyone supposed they would make a match of it. Even Gwynne? Her manner to him had never been possessive, but if her family and all of her friends believed that an understanding existed between them, might not she as well?

It was as he said: he could not help what others thought, but he had known for a very long time now that the Madocs assumed it was all but a settled thing and he had never said so much as a word to counter it. It had certainly been more comfortable to say nothing, and then, it might have come to pass in some distant future. Now there was no possibility of that; did it satisfy honor to say he had never spoken of marriage to her or her family? He feared it did not. The code of a gentleman could be an exacting thing and no respecter of a man's private feelings. He wondered if he could live up to this standard; he wondered if it mattered more to him than losing all his happiness.

Fortunately, these musings, which were conducive to nothing but a depression of the spirits, were brought to an end by the timely arrival of his brother.

"I've seen more cheerful countenances on gallows' bait," Laurie said in the way of a greeting. "Some crop or other fail? The livestock come down with some dread disease? Let's hear the worst of it," he added in a cajoling tone. Laurie's interest in the land went no further than hunting; his principal understanding of estate management was that if times were hard, his allowance was cut. So when his brother did not reply, and if anything looked glummer than ever, his concern quickened. "Is it bad, Rhys? Shall we have to retrench?"

Rhys smiled slightly. "Not at all. Why do you assume that any misfortune would be financial? In fact, from one point of view it may be the reverse. I have had word this morning that our Uncle Trefor is not expected to live out this day. I'm going to Cardiff and will stay there until that happens or he recovers this latest attack. I have only waited to tell you and ask if you wish to come with me."

Laurie lowered his cup of coffee. "And *that* is why you look so blue-deviled? If I were you I would scarcely be able to contain my excitement."

"You think the imminent death of our uncle is cause for elation?"

"No, of course not, though it would be hypocritical to pretend there was feeling on either side with the old gentleman. He was a hermit by choice. Now you shall be Lord Trefor with likely a tidy fortune."

"Or nothing at all but an empty title," Rhys pointed out. "Who knows what he did with his money after he sold everything off when he came into the title. There is no tangible thing for me to inherit like an entailed estate."

"What the devil was there for him to spend it on? He seldom went out, never had any one in; if he lived high, he did it quieter than any man I ever heard of. Probably has the lot safely tucked away in the funds."

"Probably," Rhys agreed absently.

"What is it then?" At Rhys's puzzled look, Laurie sighed with exasperation. "Why do you look like you're sitting for a study of gloom?"

Rhys only smiled at him and said, "If you mean to come with me, you had best ring for your man to pack a few things for you. We shall probably stay there for a few days to save the expense of traveling."

"You may not have to pinch pennies much longer," Laurie said, but not to be moved from his curiosity, added, "Is it a woman?"

"A woman?" Rhys looked genuinely startled.

"I know you don't spend a lot of time on *chéres amies* but, well, it can't be Gwynne, can it? She's not the sort to lead a man to merry dance and there is no obstacle there, if anything, rather less of one if you are to be Lord Trefor."

It struck Rhys forcefully that even his brother should consider his betrothal to Gwynne a certain thing. "No it is not Gwynne," he replied, and added, though not unkindly, "There are more things to life than money and women."

Laurie responded with a grin. "I know. There are also horses and cards."

This sally was successful and Rhys's features lightened. He returned his brother's smile and then rang for the traveling carriage to be prepared without satisfying Laurie's curiosity as to the cause of his bedevilment.

Catelyn too found herself frequently falling into brown studies that day. Even if she could have confided in Gwynne, she could not have confided this latest of her difficulties.

The Trefor brothers had been expected to dine that

evening, and so word was sent around to Madoc Hall of their journey to Cardiff. Catelyn was simultaneously sorry and glad that Rhys would be away for the time. Her surprise, anger, and humiliation at discovering him to be Captain Black had passed, and she was beginning to see it as very nearly the fulfillment of her own wishes. But she still could not be certain that she believed the things he had said to her the night before, and like him, she was glad to have the time to gather her thoughts about him and all that had occurred between them without having to confront him first. She believed his assertion that he had not meant to use her or abuse the trust she had placed in him; she found she rather enjoyed dwelling on his saying that he had "had" to return to her as Captain Black. She understood the compulsion only too well.

What Catelyn had difficulty understanding was why she had felt hurt and vulnerable at his revelation and had needed to lash out at him. Perhaps she felt she had exposed herself to him while he had been safely concealed by his disguise. Perhaps Gwynne's low opinion of her affected her more than she had thought. Yet if he could still come to her, admitting the truth and wishing to pay his addresses to her in a more conventional way, his opinion obviously differed from Gwynne's. She forced herself to examine this and had to admit that though his words and actions showed he wanted her, he had not mentioned marriage.

This lowering thought had the virtue of being brief. Even when he had met her as Black, he had never taken advantage of her, and she knew he would not in honor offer *carte blanche* to a gently bred maiden whose family he regarded as friends. Yet if she could believe this, what was she to think of his assertion that he did not consider himself betrothed to Gwynne? It was considered such a settled thing in the Madoc family; yet perhaps what Rhys had said was true, it was pure assumption on the part of the Madocs with no encouragement from him.

In once sense at least, her inner turmoil was resolved. If there was one man on earth she wished to be her Captain Black, it was Rhys. His good sense, his even temperament, his dry sense of humor, his quick mind, and the daring that had permitted him to carry off the masquerade made him the ideal man for her, the best of both worlds. Her greatest fear was that she had sent him away convinced of her disgust. She was glad to have the time apart to learn her own mind, but she feared that same time might change his feelings for her. It was even possible that her words would push him into Gwynne's arms.

At midweek, they received a message from Rhys from Cardiff that his uncle had indeed died and that his uncle's solicitor had hinted that the old baron's affairs were in a tangle. Rhys expected that this would keep him in Cardiff longer than he originally planned.

Catelyn was quite cast down when this news was brought to them by Sir Thomas. And when he declared that he himself would go to Cardiff to attend the funeral, she wished with all her heart to journey with him. But of course she could not. Catelyn contented herself with sending a proper and, she hoped, sufficiently kind note of condolence, regretting only that she could not entrust to her pen the things that were in her heart.

Catelyn had watched Gwynne's reaction to the news that Rhys was now Lord Trefor. It had to mean to her that Rhys, if he wished, could now claim her as his wife, but if this stirred in Gwynne's breast the least excitement, Catelyn could not detect it. In the next day or so, she saw no hint of anticipation or any outward desire in Gwynne to begin preparing for her new life.

It became important to Catelyn to know her cousin's feelings, and though she had seldom sought out Gwynne since she had misplaced her confidence in her, Catelyn did so now. The day after Sir Thomas had gone to Cardiff, Catelyn came upon Gwynne in the small writing room just off the morning room, and though it was obvious that Gwynne was busily engaged in her correspondence. Catelyn went into the room and placed herself in a chair near the desk where Gwynne sat.

Gwynne glanced up with a welcoming smile and went back to her work, assuming that Catelyn had come in for a similar purpose. But when she saw that Catelyn had not seated herself at the desk on the other side of the room, she put down her pen and looked inquiringly at the younger woman.

"Are you writing to Rhys?" Catelyn asked leadingly.

"No, to a friend of mine in Newport," Gwynne replied readily enough.

"You must be greatly anticipating Rhys's return."

Gwynne looked mildly puzzled at this but said, "Of course I miss his company, but I imagine that his business with his uncle's estate must occupy him for some time, so I do not tease myself that we shall see him anytime soon; Papa thinks another fortnight at the least."

"That must seem a very long time to you."

"No," said Gwynne with a small laugh. "Why should it?"

Catelyn willed her voice to be casual. "Rhys is Lord Trefor now and will have what he needs to run his estate without scraping to keep himself in coats. No doubt you will be married now."

Gwynne actually looked a bit surprised at this. "I suppose that's possible. I haven't given it a great deal of thought."

Catelyn could scarcely believe this. "You haven't thought of it? Don't you wish to marry Rhys?"

Gwynne tilted her head in a considering way and after a moment said, candidly, "I haven't really thought much on that either." This time she recognized Catelyn's amazement and added, "Oh, I meant I haven't thought of it lately. Ever since I was quite young, I have known that our families wished for us to wed and I suppose now it will come to be. In any case, Rhys will be in black gloves for at least a year and a wedding is not to be thought of before that."

Her calm acceptance of this made Catelyn want to shake her. *She* could not bear to wait until she could look on his face again, hear his voice, or feel his touch, yet his likely fiancée did not seem to give a fig if he spent the whole of the year of mourning away from her.

"But in the meantime, you will no doubt wish to spend time at Llanbryth arranging the household as you would wish to have it when you are mistress of the house," Catelyn said, keeping her feelings from her voice. She stood up to leave, for she could not trust herself to keep the conversation civil much longer.

"If Rhys wishes me to, I suppose I shall," Gwynne conceded. "But in truth, I am not sure I shall find time for it. I expect I shall be kept busy in the near future when Bella finds herself confined. She has told me that she depends on me to help her when the baby arrives, for she has no experience with children and is frightened."

Catelyn was arrested by this news. "Bella is increasing? I had no idea of it."

"Well, she has only just felt absolutely certain of it and has not yet told Hu," Gwynne admitted. "She confided this to Mama only last evening and Mama told me not an hour ago. She does not wish anyone to know until she has told Hu, which she means to do tonight."

Catelyn barely managed to keep from replying that in that case Bella would have been wise not to tell her secret to any member of the Madoc family. She merely expressed her happiness for Arabella and Hu and then left her cousin to her letter.

It was a small bit of hope that if Gwynne was not impatient to wed Rhys, it would be no very bad thing if Catelyn were to do what she could to attach him to herself. Now she became impatient for his return, to set right, if she could, all misunderstandings between them. The wait made her fretful, and with every sound of carriage wheels upon the gravel drive, she anticipated the appearance of her uncle with news of Rhys and when they might expect his arrival.

12

It was Sir Thomas's intention not only to attend the funeral of the fifth Baron Trefor but also to remain in Cardiff for a few days on business of his own and to advise Rhys in settling his uncle's affairs. Catelyn regarded the return of her uncle as the herald of Rhys's coming.

The moment Sir Thomas did arrive; Catelyn went with her aunt to greet him, hoping that he might give them news of Rhys at once. When Sir Thomas came into the house, both she and Lady Madoc were surprised to see Laurence Trefor enter in his wake.

While Sir Thomas had a hug for his wife, Laurie bowed over Catelyn's hand and then turned to Lady Madoc and said, "I hope I don't inconvenience you, ma'am. I have come from Cardiff only to fetch my curricle and a few items for Rhys, and Sir Thomas was kind enough to allow me to drive with him. He has assured me that you won't mind the extra for luncheon, but if you do, please say so." It was a pretty speech, spoken with Laurie's most charming smile, and it worked its intended charm on Lady Madoc.

"I would have been furious with Tom if he had not brought you," she said, smiling. "In fact, I think it likely that his motives were most selfish, for he knew that we ladies would of all things wish to see you and hear all your news. We had only the briefest note from Rhys before Tom left."

Allowing the young man to take her arm, she started up the stairs again to the saloon where she had been sitting before their arrival. Sir Thomas, wishing to change, excused himself, and Catelyn; with no invitation, followed Lady Madoc and Laurie to hear their conversation.

As they mounted the stairs en route to the saloon, Catelyn heard that Rhys was still in Cardiff and expected to be there for some time yet. He was finding his business more time-consuming than he had expected, and instead of returning to Llanbryth to supervise the settlement of the estate, he was electing to remain in Cardiff indefinitely, hoping that way to ultimately expedite the matter.

This was hardly what Catelyn wished to hear. "Then you do not know when Rhys will be back at Llanbryth?" she asked as they entered the saloon. She sat in a gilt chair near to her aunt; Laurie sat across from them.

"No, and I don't think he knows either," Laurie responded. "I had hoped to return to London by the end of the month, but now it looks unlikely. Things are in a pretty mess. Our uncle, it turns out, was an eccentric in many ways and the least of these was the way in which he dealt with his finances."

"How do you mean?" asked Lady Madoc, who sat closest to the fire, which was lit on all but the hottest days of the year. "Don't say you have discovered that he had all his money stuffed in mattresses or buried in tins in the kitchen garden?"

Laurie smiled, but his smile was wry. "No, it isn't

that, though I'm not sure that wouldn't have made matters simpler, for at least by now we might have an idea of the extent of the estate."

"I thought Rhys said that he was dealing with his uncle's solicitor," said Lady Madoc, perplexed, for though she had no hand in the financial matters of her own family, she was not entirely ignorant of the sources and management of her husband's income and knew that he put all of his dealings in the hands of his man of business. "Surely it must be his task to hand over the estate to the new Lord Trefor as tidily as possible. Unless the man is an incompetent?"

Catelyn had risen to fetch sherry for them and she now handed a glass to Laurie, who murmured his thanks to her before replying. "Mr. Jones is far from incompetent. My uncle, as his way of life attested, was an odd man, who apparently amused himself by indulging in a number of unadvised investments."

"Oh, dear!" interjected Lady Madoc. "And lost most of it, I suppose."

"Not exactly. Some proved good and some not, as might be expected, but the truth is, the estate was not nearly as extensive as Rhys believed. We may still come across a paying investment or two, or even a few that are draining, but Rhys thinks most of my uncle's affairs are, at the least, discovered now and what there is is what we can expect."

"He must be terribly disappointed," Catelyn said.

Laurie shrugged. "Rhys does not care for money the way most of us do," he said, and it was clear from his tone that he did not entirely understand this. "It does affect him, I suppose, that he won't be able to bring Llanbryth back to what it once was, as he'd hoped to do, but as he pointed out to me, he never knew for certain that he would inherit more than the title from our uncle and so it would be foolish for him to be disappointed."

"But quite human," said Lady Madoc, who sounded rather disappointed herself.

Laurie ran a thoughtful finger down the side of his nose and laughed ruefully. "Actually, I think I was the one with expectations. I'd always hoped that if I couldn't persuade Uncle Trefor to leave me a portion of his blunt, there would be enough for Rhys to share a bit with me after he took care of Llanbryth."

He drank off the last of his wine and turned to Catelyn with an engaging grin. "It would seem I shall have to find and marry an heiress after all. Are you quite sure you won't have me, Cat? We could make it a double wedding when Rhys marries Gwynne."

He spoke lightly, having no idea of the effect of his words on Catelyn. She was spared having to answer by the arrival of Gwynne and Bella, who at once plied Laurie with questions about Rhys's inheritance and about his friends in Cardiff. After a while Sir Thomas joined them again, and when Hu came in from the stables after a ride into the village, they went into luncheon, a meal which gave great credit to Lady Madoc's cook's ability to handle an unexpected guest with no notice.

Lady Madoc did what she could to persuade Laurie to remain with them for the rest of the afternoon, but he insisted that he had to return to Cardiff that same evening.

"But it is quite late," Gwynne said to him. "If you are first to go to Llanbryth and have errands to do there before you leave, it will probably be near dark before you are back in Cardiff."

Laurie was glad of her concern but hastened to assure her that it was necessary. "I have an excellent team and the drive won't take me much above two hours. In any case, the moon has not completely waned, and I shall have a bit of light from it to guide me if I am delayed in my start for Cardiff."

"If you must leave that late, you would do best to remain the night," Lady Madoc told him. "It is always dangerous to travel that far in the dark, and there is always the danger of brigands."

Laurie smiled. "I don't mean to let that worry me. No one has heard a thing from that fellow Cat and I surprised holding up the carriage since that day. Rank amateur if you ask me and gone to ground. Probably for good."

"Perhaps he's waiting for a pot worthy of his stature," suggested Hu.

"Exactly the thinking of Lord Tremaine," said Sir Thomas, nodding. "Do as Bess says, boy. Go while it's light or stay the night at Llanbryth. Or here, if you want company."

Laurie thanked him and said he was sure he would be able to manage an early enough start to avoid any dangers. But, curious, he added, "*Is* Tremaine expecting a highwayman to strike his quarterly shipment of coin for his mines? On the basis of that one incident?" Lord Tremaine was also a magistrate and Laurence had always regarded him as a man of great sense, despite his silly wife. "Or does he have other information?"

"No, no," Sir Thomas assured him. "It is just that he wishes to be cautious. Most rumors have some basis and he sees no harm in taking precautions."

"I suppose he means to put on an extra guard," said Laurie.

"Tremaine is too tightfisted for that," said Hu caustically. "He has decided to be clever. Instead of paying another man with a pistol, he means to rouse the usual ones out of their beds at an ungodly hour to throw a potential thief off his stride. Who would expect a shipment of gold to go out before dawn?"

"Who indeed?" said Laurie dryly. "No doubt the secrecy of the plan will assure its success," he added, but this was lost on all in the room except Catelyn. Laurie caught her eye and they exchanged a knowing smile.

Laurie then left them with a number of messages for his brother and a letter to carry to Arabella's parents informing them of the forthcoming birth of their first grandchild. This he promised most faithfully to deliver by hand so that he might return and relate to Bella the happy countenances of her mother and father when they discovered the news.

After her initial anticipation that she would soon see Rhys again, Catelyn was quite cast down to learn that he would be away even longer than expected. Her impatience to see him was rapidly turning to frustration. It even occurred to her in this unhappy state that he was willfully staying away from Llanbryth to avoid her. The short distance of his estate from Cardiff would not have made his returning there impossible if he had wished to be home and she argued with herself that if he truly desired to be with her, he might have found it not so very inconvenient to do so.

But as it happened, she had little time to dwell on these things before she saw him again. The very next morning she received a letter from her father. Her discovery of Captain Black's identity had helped to erase from her mind her written request to leave Madoc, and so when his letter came it was almost a surprise—and not a very pleasant one.

It was not that her father remained hard and unforgiving; quite the reverse, he stated that he would be most glad to see his beloved daughter soon and that as he had business in the area at the end of the month, he thought he might as well come to visit his sister, whom he had not seen in a number of years, and at the same time collect his daughter and return with her to their home in Brighton.

The unaccustomed kindness of the letter showed Catelyn that her father had not only forgiven her for her scandalous behavior but was perhaps a bit sorry for his harsh treatment. Two months ago the letter would have filled her with joy, two weeks ago it would at least have brought her relief, now it did neither.

It was less than a fortnight to the end of the month, and for all Catelyn knew, Rhys would not return to Llanbryth before that time. She did not know that seeing Rhys again would assure her future happiness; it might do quite the reverse, but she knew that she positively could not leave Madoc Hall without talking with him again. If this proved impossible because he did not return to Llanbryth, she would find some means of going to him in Cardiff.

That night she planted the first seed of her plan by remarking to her aunt that she had not visited Cardiff since the assembly. As an added incentive, she also mentioned to Bella that she would doubtless wish to visit with her parents soon. Lady Madoc only replied that she was sure they would manage this in the fortnight ahead, but without making any definite plan for it, and Bella, cryptically, but encouragingly, responded that she had reason to hope that she would soon be spending far more of her time in Cardiff.

Catelyn was content enough with this response, and with her schemes to occupy her mind, she retired that night as nearly untroubled as she had been since the night she had thought to stroll in the garden and had found herself in the old gatehouse in the arms of a strange man.

Catelyn slept well and the following morning she was late rising. But reaching the breakfast room, she found the entire family still seated at table. It was plain to her at once from the set of their countenances that there was something afoot.

Sir Thomas looked troubled and angry, Lady Madoc's brow was creased with concern, Hu stood by the fireplace kicking at stray coals in a distracted way, Arabella sat uncommonly quiet with something very near to a pout marring her lovely features. Only Gwynne maintained her usual bearing and it was she alone who seemed to take note of Catelyn's tardy entrance.

Catelyn returned her greeting and sat down in her usual place. She poured herself a cup of chocolate and waited for someone to tell her what had happened, but the room was pregnant with their silence. "Is something the matter?" she asked when she could bear it no longer.

"You have not heard the news from your maid?" said Lady Madoc, surprised. "I am sure the servants are doing far more gossiping than working today."

"No. Though it did seem to me that Annie was extraordinarily quiet," Catelyn said, remembering this. "She was displeased with me last night because I would not heed her advice on which gown to wear to dinner and I thought it was just that, so I did not encourage her."

"No doubt she did not wish to distress you," Gwynne suggested.

"Is this something to do with me?" Catelyn was so surprised that she spilled her chocolate. "Please tell me, Cousin, for I am beginning to imagine horrors."

It was Bella who spoke. "The man that you met who calls himself Captain Black is a real highwayman, Cat. His robbery was successful this time and there is no doubt of his identity. He has robbed Lord Tremaine's coin and gold and has shot one of the guards hired to protect it."

Catelyn was mopping at the spill with her napkin but again her action was arrested. "You know Captain Black did this? How can that be?" She turned to her uncle and said almost accusingly, "You assured me, sir, that there was not really such a man. I don't believe the man I met at the gatehouse was really a highwayman and you yourself agreed that the robbery Laurie and I witnessed was an amateurish thing."

"I have never thought that there was just one man and I still don't," said Sir Thomas. "Doubtless it is as I have said, someone is using the legend for his advantage. Dressed up like a theater version of a highwayman this time, from the report we had, and making sure that all heard his voice and that his accent was educated."

"That can be imitated," Hu pointed out.

"As likely as not it was," Gwynne said practically. Of all those present, she alone maintained her usual serenity. Frankly, Catelyn did not see why the robbery of Lord Tremaine should give everyone such

Friday faces, and why it should be assumed that she would be distressed as well.

"The worst of it, of course," said Lady Madoc mournfully, "is that he has doubtless been using our property as a place to hide and to plan his crime. It happened near to us again where our property meets the Cardiff road, and the witnesses said that he disappeared into the woods of Llanbryth, which you know marches exactly along our property line."

"There is no blame to you in this, of course," Sir Thomas said kindly to Catelyn, which puzzled her very much. "You could not know the danger involved, though keeping such information to yourself was ill-advised."

"To think that Captain Black actually came into our own garden." Arabella gave a faint and not unpleasurable shiver. "I for one am glad I did not know of it."

Catelyn's understanding was not inferior and her puzzlement gave way to a sense of betrayal. She looked to her aunt, who avoided her eyes.

"You must not blame your Aunt Bess," Sir Thomas said, understanding. "When we heard the news, she knew she had to tell me all, though she did not like to break your confidence."

"I am sorry, Uncle," Catelyn said, though she felt far more angry than contrite. "I know I should not have encouraged that man to come into the garden." She paused hoping her aunt had not felt obliged to confide *every* detail of those meetings. "But I feel certain that this was someone masquerading for his own amusement. I cannot believe he could be the same man who robbed Lord Tremaine."

"Of course it was," said Hu impatiently. He came over to the table and sat down in his chair in a pettish way. "Do you suppose dressing up as highwaymen is a neighborhood pastime?"

Catelyn had no answer for this; she knew if she could tell them the truth about Captain Black, they would understand. To believe there were not two men posing as the highwayman was to believe that Rhys had taken to the High Toby, which was absurd. "Did you not just say, Uncle, that you believed there was more than one man claiming to be Captain Black?"

But it was Hu who answered her again. "Given the circumstances," he said scornfully, "that is unlikely."

"I don't see that," Catelyn retorted. She particularly disliked it when Hu used that tone of pronouncement with her.

"Of course you cannot like thinking that the man you met was truly a criminal," Lady Madoc said to her niece, "but I do think Hu must be right. He did use the gatehouse just as the legend says he did and it was exactly here that he held up the cart carrying the gold."

Catelyn wanted to point out that it must be a very stupid highwayman who would choose to perpetrate his crime at Madoc if everyone knew that he would be there. No matter, if was clear to her that they all believed the man she had met and the highwayman were the same. In fairness to them, she knew that if Rhys had not revealed himself to her, she might well have believed it herself.

"I still think it is most unfair to say that now we may not go to Cardiff, *belle-mère*," Bella said. She did not care much about the robbery, and expressed no curiosity in knowing the actual perpetrator. "Catelyn is wishful to go as well, and I particularly wish to speak to my mama and papa."

"And so you shall, my dear," said Sir Thomas patiently, making it clear that this was not the first time he had said so. "The moment the devil is caught or that we can ascertain that he no longer lurks in the neighborhood, you shall have your visit."

"You know highwaymen are seldom caught," Arabella said pettishly. "You have said so yourself."

"But my love," Lady Madoc said soothingly, "surely you would not even wish to venture out on that road knowing that such a desperate creature is about. This is twice he has struck and we can no longer ignore the danger. Never fear, Sir Thomas and Lord Tremaine are organizing the neighborhood, and even if he has gone to ground, they shall soon route him or at the very lease frighten him away."

Something about this speech made Catelyn suspect that her aunt was repeating Sir Thomas or even Hu. But the news that there was not to be any trips into Cardiff was a blow to her. Now she truly did feel affected by the events of the morning.

Like Bella she did not care a fig for the actual robbery. She was sorry that a man had been shot, but he was apparently in no great danger and Lord Tremaine was rich enough to bear the loss without hardship. It was obvious to Catelyn that her plan of the previous evening would no longer suffice and she would have to think of a way to convince her aunt and uncle of the safety and felicity of venturing into Cardiff if Rhys did not return soon.

"In any case," Catelyn said, making a beginning, "it is unlikely that we would be molested, for we would have no attractions for a highwayman. Surely you cannot mean that we are to stay in the house for an indefinite time?"

"That is exactly what they mean," said Bella with a

heavy sigh. "We are not even to go into the village without escort or to ride out of the estate."

"It is for your own good," her husband admonished. "Robbery is one thing, but there has been a brandishing of pistols, and if this is a man of violence, we cannot have women risking an encounter."

"No doubt he will draw his pistol to demand our lacquer beads," Catelyn said sardonically. The entire situation was becoming melodrama. "I know of no woman who wears fine jewels for country morning visits or shopping in the village."

"Two men were shot, Cat," Gwynne said quietly. "That is a fact that cannot be denied and which we must take most seriously, whatever the personal sacrifice."

"Two men?" said Cat. "I thought you said it was only the guard?"

"The guard feels certain that he winged the highwayman," Hu explained. "He was fired on before he shot the guard himself and both witnesses claim that the bandit staggered at one point and nearly lost his balance when he remounted his horse."

"Then if he is a gentleman highwayman, look among your acquaintances for someone with a recent injury and you shall have your bravo," Catelyn suggested.

But this was met by protests from Sir Thomas and Lady Madoc that they would not believe such a thing of a man gently bred, a comment from Gwynne that this would put in jeopardy every man who had had a toss from his horse, and Bella again took up her lament that it seemed unjust to her that she should be forbidden to visit her parents at such a particular time.

With all this going on about her, Catelyn never did get much breakfast beyond her dish of chocolate and some dry toast with marmalade, but she was not really hungry. She was more occupied with trying to think how she would manage to see Rhys and settle things between them before her father returned.

When the servant who took the day's correspondence into the village for posting returned with letters for the family, Arabella at least no longer felt the ill effects of the restrictions placed upon her. She received a letter from her father, which put her in such a happy state of mind that she had no thought for anything else.

Arabella was with Catelyn in the still room when she read the letter, and it was obvious to Catelyn that the news was most pleasing. But beyond exclaiming that her papa was the best of all possible fathers, she did not disclose the contents of her letter, and went off at once in search of her husband.

Catelyn did not see Bella again until she went up to her room to dress for dinner and found the younger woman waiting for her. "Oh, Cat," she said joyously as they entered Catelyn's bedchamber together, "it is the most famous thing. Papa says that if we still wish to have our own establishment in Cardiff, he will buy a house for us as a christening present for our child. Only we must have it at once so that I may have my confinement in town."

Catelyn was very happy for Bella, for she knew how much the young woman missed her life in the city, and though she herself had adjusted well to the slower pace of country life, she could well understand Bella's feelings.

It was soon clear to her, though, that this mattered to Bella mostly because it mattered to Hu. "He has always wished this of all things," she confided, "and when I wrote to Papa to tell him that I was increasing,

I hinted that this would be a good thing for us and that I wished to have my child in Cardiff to be near a good physician instead of having to rely on the village midwife. I think this will be very good for Hu; he has had such odd humors of late. I do not at all understand it, for he was the sweetest-tempered man I have ever known."

This was not Catelyn's opinion of Hu Madoc, but she allowed for the fact that he was viewed quite differently by his wife. "He should certainly be happy now, for even I have heard him say how much he wishes you might live in Cardiff at least a part of the year."

For the first time Bella's features clouded. "You know, it is the strangest thing, but he did not seem nearly as pleased as I thought he would. I mean, he is very glad of it, but he said we must not rush into anything and that it would be as well to wait awhile before going into Cardiff to look for the house. I rather thought he would forget these silly restraints about traveling and have the carriage for the morning."

Bella was sitting in a chair next to Catelyn; who was sitting at her dressing table, taking pins from her hair. Catelyn gave her a reassuring smile through the glass. "He and Sir Thomas have decided to be most cautious since Lord Tremaine was robbed. I, too think it is overdone and absurd, but you know how men can be at times, especially when they think they are doing something for one's own good. And you know," she added encouragingly, "Hu has been most busy of late helping my uncle with the management of the estate." But there was no need for him to dampen her enthusiasm, Catelyn added, but not aloud, for she would not for the world have hurt her new friend.

Bella was glad enough to snatch at this excuse for

her husband and chattered on quite happily about the manner of house they would purchase and the hangings she would select for it until it was time for her to dress as well.

13

With Hu and Arabella's plans still uncertain, the constant speculation on the robbery, and the usual activities of country life, the next fortnight passed far more quickly than Catelyn had hoped it would. Her own difficulties remained unresolved. Rhys had yet to return to Llanbryth and she had been unable to put forth any scheme that would take her to him.

Her father was expected in three days, and even if he was persuaded to remain for longer than the sennight he planned, she feared she would not see Rhys before she left Wales.

But Catelyn was not a young woman to let circumstances rule her fate. The only thing she could think to do was to write Rhys, telling him that she was soon to return to her father and that she felt there was unfinished business between them. This sounded simple enough in theory, but when she sat down at one of the two desks in the writing room, she found she spent more of her time mending her pen than writing with it.

The difficulty was that all *was* unresolved between them. Their last meeting had been upsetting and confusing and by the time she had gotten over the shock and sorted out her feelings, he was gone. He had implied that he loved her, but that was not the same as the words being spoken. She teased herself with this concern so much that the end result was a vague and unassuming letter, which Catelyn thought as she read it over, left room to doubt whether she wished him to return to Llanbryth at once or remain in Cardiff until she had left the neighborhood.

In the end, she sealed it, and directed it anyway, deciding that if he did care for her he would understand, and if he did not, then it hardly mattered.

She took the letter downstairs to put it with the others to be taken into the village, but it was destined never to leave the house. Her uncle's news at lunch made sending it unnecessary.

"We can expect to greet Rhys as the new Lord Trefor tomorrow," he reported as he suspiciously inspected a dainty cucumber sandwich. "That's certainly good news for one member of this family," he added with a knowing wink at Gwynne.

Needless to say, Catelyn's reaction to this was mixed. She was elated at the first part and disliked being reminded of the second. Gwynne smiled slightly at her father but otherwise did not appear to find the news especially heartening. Catelyn thought her a fool yet envied her at the same time.

The source of Sir Thomas's news was the bailiff of Llanbryth who had told Sir Thomas's own agent over a glass of heavy wet the night before in Taff Wyd that he expected to see his master on the morrow. This meant that Rhys might already be at Llanbryth and that she would probably see him the very next day at Madoc Hall. Catelyn felt relieved and a little anxious as well.

"It would seem," Sir Thomas continued when the murmurs and comments quieted, "that Rhys is finally straightened out the biggest mess of confounding paper that I've ever seen. From what his man told Adams, matters have worked out better for him than he first believed. I don't know that I'll be the father of the grandest lady in the neighborhood," he added, still determined to quiz his daughter, "but I'll wager you can put aside any fears that Laurie might have caused you that you'd be forever scraping pennies."

Lady Madoc was quite animated. "Do you mean that Laurie was mistaken, Tom? Is Rhys's inheritance less meager than he feared?"

"So I gather," said Sir Thomas, draining his cup of tea as if it were medicine. "From what Adams was told, Trefor has given his agent the office to order any amount of equipment to bring Llanbryth up to the level of a paying estate."

"At least we have had news of someone finding money instead of having it taken away from them," Lady Madoc said.

Sir Thomas laughed. "If Rhys were not Rhys and the unlikeliest man on earth to turn dishonest, I'd wonder if he and the thief were not related." The rest of his family smiled in response, but Catelyn felt an icy chill, as ridiculous to her as it was frightening. She knew that Rhys could not have taken his masquerade to that length, whatever Hu might have said about the unlikeliness of two Captain Blacks existing. The unexpected size of his inheritance could only be coincidental. She knew her fear that he might have taken to the bridle lay to find the money for Llanbryth to assuage his disappointment was absurd.

The next day she hurried through breakfast in anticipation of a morning call from Rhys and was dispirited and restless at luncheon when he had still not come to Madoc Hall. It was Saturday and her

father was expected on Monday or Tuesday. She knew
Rhys was sure to come before that time, but she could
scarcely curb her impatience.

After luncheon was ended, she had planned to go
with Gwynne and Lady Madoc to give the rector the
completed altar linens, but at the last minute she cried
off and, donning her riding habit, went to the stables.

The groom had been instructed to accompany the
ladies of the house on their rides, but Catelyn assured
the undergroom, the same one she had once before
persuaded to her wishes, that she did not mean to ride
beyond the park, and thus escaped the chaperon.

This was not true, but the lie did not especially
trouble her conscience, for she did not mean to leave
the estate entirely. She left the stable at a sedate walk
until she had skirted the house and then she headed
onto a path that led to the northern border of the
estate, which, as it happened, marched with the land
of the new Lord Trefor.

A plan of what she would do when she reached the
boundaries was not precisely formed in Catelyn's
mind. She did not assume that by going to the edge of
Rhys's property she must surely encounter him, but she
did not dismiss the possibility either. Better to do
something rather than sit about the house fretting
away the afternoon, she told herself.

Catelyn reached the edge of Madoc sooner than she
had expected. Not surprisingly, all she saw besides the
property marker that Sir Thomas had long ago erected
was more wood. It was not difficult to convince herself
to continue on, and when she reached the end of the
wood, she faced the Llanbryth park. She did not turn
around as her sensible self urged her to do, but proceeded on, skirting the edge of the wood until the rose
garden came into view. Catelyn did not let herself

think of what she was doing as she crossed the grassy expanse, nor did she think of what she would do when she finally reached the house.

The obvious course was to ride around to the front of the house, ring the bell like a proper guest, and ask to see him. If she had any certainty of his feelings for her she might have done just that, but she felt overcome with an uncharacteristic shyness.

The only other thing she could think to do was to tether her horse and to walk into the garden, hoping to find him in his study with the garden door open to the beauty of the day. She did not know what she would say to him when he righteously demanded to know what she was doing lurking in his garden.

This time she was in luck. The door to the study *was* open and she heard both Rhys and Laurie's voices. She waited, hoping that Laurie would leave, but after a while she began to weary of the wait and knew that if she were not back at Madoc soon there would be alarm. Having come this far, she could not simply leave, and taking her courage in both hands, she did the only thing she could do. She mounted the two stone stairs and walked into the room.

The two men were seated at the opposite end of the room. Rhys was at a writing desk and Laurie in a chair beside him. They were in deep conversation and did not immediately notice her.

"I think it is foolish," Laurie was saying, while he absently played with the cap of the standish. "If you do not take care of your arm, you may injure it far worse and then where will you be?"

"At least I will not be taken up as a highwayman," Rhys said dryly.

"That is nonsense and you know it. A stupid rumor is no reason to hide an injury. Your arm gives you pain when you lift it; it should be bound to keep it steady."

"There is more to this than you know."

"What is . . ." Laurie at last caught sight of Catelyn and broke off. He started for the briefest moment and then recovering his usual composure, he touched Rhys gently.

Rhys turned to see what had surprised Laurie, and his own eyes widened for a moment before becoming veiled. Catelyn, for her part, felt even more uncomfortable than she had thought she would. "I-I saw the door open and came in," she stammered, and was angry with herself for looking so foolish. "I didn't mean to interrupt—I didn't think. Perhaps I should go."

Both young men had risen from their chairs and Catelyn had noticed that Rhys did so somewhat carefully, keeping his left arm still. His expression and his voice revealed nothing of his feelings. "Please stay. I am glad you have thought to stop on your ride, and in any case, you do not interrupt, for Laurie was just about to leave."

It was clear to Catelyn, though Laurie's surprise was scarcely manifest, that it was the first notion he had of this. Addressing him, Rhys added, "Please pull the bell for me on the way out, Laurie."

Whatever Laurie thought of all this, he was as good as his brother at keeping his thoughts to himself. But Catelyn thought she noticed speculation when he looked to her and then to his brother. "Of course, Rhys," he said affably. "And if I pass Thymes, I'll just tell him to fetch the sherry, shall I? You have sufficient brandy here, haven't you?"

"Sherry will do nicely," Rhys said flatly.

Catelyn had stopped a few feet from the brothers. Laurie walked over to her and took her hand, a smile in his eyes. "I'll see you tonight, fair one. We dine at Madoc." Then he threw a glance over his shoulder at Rhys that was decidedly provocative. Rhys's smile was dry.

Catelyn watched this brief exchange, aware of an uncomfortable warmth. She could well guess what Laurie was thinking, could not at all guess what Rhys thought; and was herself unsure of the thoughts that chased each other in her own head.

When Laurie had left them, Rhys did not resume his seat at the desk but led Catelyn to a spindle-legged sofa that had a comfortable used look. "I *am* glad to see you, Catelyn," he said, and she thought his tone was guarded. "Do you bring me messages from Madoc? Lady Madoc hasn't decided to put off dinner to-night?"

"No, in fact, I didn't know you would be with us tonight," she said truthfully, but knew she might have guessed it if she had been thinking clearly. She twisted her riding crop in her hands and said awkwardly, "I *was* passing and thought to stop."

"Should I be flattered?" he said, but there was no sarcasm at all in his voice. "You have gotten over your shock of discovering me to be Captain Black, I take it. Do you mean to forgive me then, and believe that I never meant to use you or abuse your trust in me?"

Catelyn found meeting his eyes, which were discouragingly unexpressive, surprisingly difficult. She studied the brown twist of leather in her hands as if it were an important thing. "There is nothing to forgive," she said a trifle gruffly. "I was surprised . . . I don't know why I reacted so extremely. Perhaps it was the shock of it. I mean the way you did it, coming up on me in the dark. I had just been thinking, you see . . ."

"What had you been thinking?" he prompted when she did not go on after a moment or two.

Catelyn made herself look at him. "That dash and boldness were not perhaps desirable qualities in a man. That . . . that there are other things more important and lastingly attractive." She finished the last in a rush, which made the silence that followed seem much longer than it actually was.

"I see," he said quietly at last. "Then I disappointed you in quite a different way."

"Yes. No. That is, I was astonished and confused. I thought I knew you, but I did not. It made me say things . . ." Her eyes pleaded for encouragement; she had never guessed how difficult it would be to speak her heart, but his own eyes remained veiled and his features, though not set, were unyielding. The fears that had plagued her, that she had given him a permanent disgust of her, loomed very real, and defensively, she began to feel angry for his want of response. "It made me say things that were ill-considered and of the moment," she said with better composure. "I beg your pardon for it."

"That is generous of you," he said with equal formality.

Catelyn's last hope for a happy ending to her romance with Captain Black dissipated. Perhaps he desired her, but he could not love her and be so cold when he must guess what she was trying to say. It was really only at this moment that she realized the full extent of her wish for his love. Her heart desired to pour itself out to him, to beg him to love her if need be, but her pride, in the face of his unresponsiveness, forbade this.

So she pushed her feelings aside and looked to the anger his hurtfulness caused to her. Before she could speak again the butler came in with a decanter and two glasses. When it was set down and the butler had bowed himself out of the room, she coolly declined the proffered refreshment. "I think I had best return to Madoc; I am unattended, and if my aunt returns from her visit to the rectory before I am home, she will worry."

"I suppose she has insisted that you take a groom when you ride and that you have ignored the restriction," he said with the nearest thing to a smile that he had offered since her arrival. "You should take care, Cat. What happened to Tremaine's quarterly wages for his mines was not a romantic masquerade. It may be dangerous for you to go about unescorted."

Catelyn stood and favored him with a caustic smile. "I was given to understand that you and your brethren are creatures of the night."

"I fancy that may be true only for bogus highwaymen," he replied as he stood with her. "This real one appears to heed no such restrictions."

"Assuming the bogus and the real to be separate men."

His eyes opened completely at this and he laughed. "Are you supposing that I put on my guise as Black and forced the cart to stand and deliver?"

"Hu thinks it extremely unlikely that there would be two men in exactly the same place playing the same game."

"You don't really believe this, Cat." It was more statement than question. "Why ever would I do such a thing?"

"For the money, of course; isn't that the usual reason? Laurie told us how little your uncle's estate brought you."

"He was mistaken." She raised her brows in disbelief which made him add, "I have been poor for some time. If I were going to embark upon a career of crime to line my pockets, I would have done so when I came into Llanbryth and thus saved myself three years of privation."

"Perhaps you have only wearied of it now."

"Perhaps I decided that Laurie was in the right of it and wanted the means to maintain a position worthy of the Four Horse Club," he said mockingly.

There was no real seriousness in Catelyn's mind about the accusation she made. She knew Rhys was not a thief—or at least not a thief of gold. Once again in her hurt she lashed out at him with the only weapon at hand. "There is also the little matter of your injury which you told Laurie you wish to hide," she reminded him coldly.

He looked taken aback for a moment and then said, "Ah, yes. I was forgetting that you had overheard that. I have heard the rumor that the highwayman was wounded and I wished to keep small minds from big imaginings. It is not such a glamorous wound, only a small hurt caused by my own carelessness and my late uncle's taste for clutter."

She felt the stinging insult of his words. "Logical progression of thought and pettiness of mind are not the same," she said angrily.

"It is when the assumption is invalid in the first place," he retorted, beginning to sound angry.

"*If* it is." Her eyes flashed sparks of ice. "Because of your masquerade, everyone was half expecting the return of Black. The opportunity to play the part could never have been better."

"I wonder that you stand so accusing when it was the image of the highwayman that so attracted you," he said with an unpleasant curl to his lips. "I wonder that you can find the strength to keep from throwing yourself at my head if you really believe me to be the highwayman."

"Whatever you are, you are no gentleman," she said with fury. "How dare you say that to me? I can see what value you place on me; you would never speak so to Gwynne."

"Gwynne would make it unnecessary."

This could not have affected her more if he had actually struck her. Almost reflexively, her own hand flashed to hit him, but he was quicker and caught her arm at the wrist. He held her firmly for a long moment, their eyes locked in silent battle. It came hard to her, but in the end she submitted to his superior strength. She dropped her eyes and in response he dropped his arm.

Without saying another word or even looking at him, she quickly gathered the trailing skirts of her habit, turned, and left the room by the way she had come. Her eyes stung and her throat felt parched, but she did not give in to her overwhelming desire to weep until she was completely certain of being alone.

14

Not surprisingly, after seeing Rhys, Catelyn again was glad of her father's imminent arrival and her removal from Madoc Hall. She knew this was a capriciousness born of her unbridled emotions, and though she hated herself for it, she was powerless to help it.

What had happened to the cool, serene, sophisticated young woman who had come to Wales regarding her banishment as a temporary setback to the complete control she had of her life? Hadn't she thwarted the best efforts of her father and Aunt Philippa to command her life as they saw fit? Now it seemed she could not even prevail against herself. One moment she hoped with all her heart never to even see Rhys again and the next she wanted some miracle to bring them together.

Catelyn dreaded the thought of meeting him at dinner, but the pride that would not let her beg for his regard would also not now allow her to be craven and pretend to be ill. As some semblance of calm returned to her, she realized that nothing between them was different. What she mourned for now was something that had never existed.

In all too short a time, Rhys and Laurie arrived for dinner. Lady Madoc was in bustling high spirits; she fully expected that before the evening was out her only daughter would be formally promised in marriage.

Catelyn could not resist looking up at Rhys when he first came into the dining room, and as soon as he had greeted his hostess, his eyes found hers. But the gaze was perfunctory, and the small bow of acknowledgment was dictated by no more than politeness.

Rhys did not earn his meal that night with entertaining conversation any more than Catelyn did. Even Laurie was less than his usually cheerful self. The conversation was left to Lady Madoc and Bella, who discussed the move to Cardiff and Bella's approaching motherhood at exhausting lengths.

"You know, Bella," Hu said irritably near the end of the meal, "you are not the first woman to find yourself in this condition. I am sure it is all very interesting, but you don't want to become one of those boring matrons who have no other conversation."

Catelyn thought this unnecessarily cruel. Bella lived for her husband's pleasures, which must at times be tiresome, and now after a year of plying her needle and discussing household management with her mother-in-law, she at last had something to absorb her and give her some importance in her own eyes.

"It is far more interesting and entertaining a subject for conversation than blood sports," Catelyn said pointedly to Hu, who was fond, when the family dined alone, of discussing his shooting and hunting accomplishments in lavish detail. "And it is certainly preferable to eating in silence." She was not sure what had made her say this last, for she was as guilty as any of the others, but the effect was remarkable. Almost at once the conversation picked up dramatically.

The interminal dinner was at last brought to an end, and the moment the ladies retired to the withdrawing room Lady Madoc began discussing the topic that was truly first in her thoughts, but which could not be mentioned in the presence of the Trefors: whether or not Rhys would choose this night to offer for Gwynne.

"Depend upon it, my love," Lady Madoc told her daughter, "that is why he is so thoughtful tonight. He is no doubt rehearsing what he will say to Papa."

When the gentlemen came into the room, it was not just Laurie and Hu as the women had expected, but Rhys and Sir Thomas as well. Catelyn, on the watch for such a thing, saw Lady Madoc search her husband's expression for confirmation of her hopes, and she saw the nearly imperceptible shake of Sir Thomas's head.

While watching this, she did not notice that Rhys had chosen the chair next to hers. She had deliberately placed herself a bit apart from the others in the corner of the room, for she did not wish to be a conspicuous part of the circle which must first congratulate the happy couple. She doubted her ability to maintain her equanimity to that extent. She was surprised that Rhys should first come to her but knew that sooner or later she would have to speak with him again and it was best to have it over with.

"I wished to apologize to you," he said stiffly. "I shouldn't have said the things I did today."

"It was not without provocation," she said quietly. She looked up at him from her needlework and felt her heart move. She quickly looked away again.

"*Is* what you said today what you think of me?" he asked.

No, I don't despise you, I love you, she heard herself say, but it was only in her head. In actuality she only shook her head. He said nothing and after a moment he left her in response to a summons from Lady Madoc. A few minutes later, he rose again and exchanged a few quiet words with Sir Thomas, then he and the older man left the room. Catelyn watched this scene with a leaden heart. Her mind was so far from her work that she set any number of wrong stitches and finally gave up her work, picked up a book in order to avoid conversation, and pretended to read.

Laurie came to sit beside her in the chair Rhys had occupied. "Difficult passage?"

She did not understand him. "Difficult?"

"You haven't turned a page for a full quarter hour."

She replied without thinking. "They haven't been gone that long."

"Rhys and Sir Thomas," Laurie said sagely. "I thought that was it."

"What was it?"

"I'm not a fool, you know. And there had to be some reason why you didn't succumb to my fatal charm."

In spite of everything, Laurie made her smile. "I can guess what you are thinking because of my odd visit to Llanbryth this afternoon. You are mistaken."

"I don't think so," he said, and after a thoughtful pause added, "I know Rhys seems a close sort of fellow, but he's not like that with me. But he won't discuss you with me, which tells all. Poor Gwynne."

"Poor Gwynne?" Catelyn said with indignant astonishment. "Rhys is with Sir Thomas now and I shall doubtless be wishing her happy before the night is over. I don't know where you find your ideas, Laurie, but you are fair and far out."

A short silence fell between them, which Laurie did not attempt to breech. He sat beside her and watched her watching Gwynne, not in the least surprised when she spoke again with something in her voice that made him feel like an eavesdropper.

"She hardly looks as if she cares."

A servant came into the room just then with a request from Sir Thomas for Gwynne to come to the study. Catelyn watched her leave with an intensity of which she was unaware.

"The thing must be settled then," she said with a brightness that sounded false even to her. To dissuade Laurie from pursuing this, she said, "It was a very good thing that Rhys was able to realize his full inheritance."

"It was good for me too," Laurie said with a laugh. "I'll come up a bit in the world because of it. I was the one who found the papers that led us to the investments which proved so lucrative, you know, and Rhys feels it is only fair that I should have a portion."

"Sufficient for you to live in London as you wish?"

He smiled slowly. "Only marrying an heiress of your magnitude would give me that. But Rhys is being most generous—better than I'd hoped for. Or deserve."

Catelyn looked at him for a long moment. "You and Rhys are more alike than I once thought," she said suddenly.

Laurie looked a bit nonplussed. "Is that a compliment or a condemnation?" he asked with an uncertain laugh.

"You know it must be a compliment."

"Rhys is the finer copy, though, isn't he?"

"I am not a fit person to ask that of," she said with a tiny catch in her voice. It felt good to admit aloud that she did care for Rhys. She didn't know if she could trust Laurie, but at this moment she did not care.

"He's a great fool if he marries Gwynne," he said,

taking her hand in his. "And I am not thinking of your dowry when I say that."

This made Catelyn smile, and she squeezed his hand in gratitude.

At last, the door opened again and Sir Thomas came in, followed by Rhys and Gwynne, who were smiling at each other and had the look of two people most content. This stabbed at Catelyn harder than anything he had ever said to her. Those in the room looked up expectantly, but Gwynne merely resumed her seat at the tapestry frame, Rhys went over to sit beside Hu and Bella, and Sir Thomas assiduously avoided meeting his wife's curious eye. There was a minute or two of anticlimatic silence before everyone began to speak again.

It was not only Lady Madoc who had difficulty not speaking the question in her mind and conversation was a bit stilted. Fortunately for the piece of mind of all, Rhys soon rose and, pleading his neglected estate business, left with Laurie in tow.

Lady Madoc impatiently cast aside the altar cloth she had been working on. "Well? Aren't you going to tell us, Gwynne? I think it was quite cruel of you and Rhys to keep us in suspense this way. How I contained myself, I cannot imagine."

Gwynne raised her eyes to her mother briefly but did not pause in her stitching. "I am glad that you did, Mama. We should all have been most uncomfortable if you had, for Rhys and I are not going to make any announcement. We shall not suit, Mama. There is to be no betrothal and I have released him from any promises that he'd made or I'd assumed."

Lady Madoc's face was a caricature of dismayed astonishment. "Not suit! Not suit! I have never heard of such a thing. Of course you will suit. I have never seen a more perfect matching. I see what it is," she said, her eyes narrowing with suspicion. "Now he is Lord Trefor with an independence and you are no longer good enough for him. Oh, this is the outside of enough! To think I have treated that man like my son already. Nourishing a viper is what I have been doing."

"Now don't excite yourself, Bess," Sir Thomas said soothingly. "It is no such thing. As it is, I do not think Gwynne is so very disappointed, are you, pet?" Gwynne bestowed one of her gentle smiles on her father and shook her head. "There, do you see?" he went on. "This has always been more our wish than that of either Gwynne or Rhys, and I must say that it would be unfair to that young man to condemn him. He spoke to me in such a way as could only do him credit.

"He said he understood that by allowing the assumption to continue for so long he felt honor bound to commit himself to Gwynne, but he admitted that he could not love her but as a sister, and when I had Gwynne come to us, she said much the same thing."

Lady Madoc looked at her daughter with reproach. "He was willing to marry you and you allowed him to cry off? Oh, my love, how could you be so foolish? If he loves you as a sister, that is far more than many marriages begin with and I know he would make you happy."

Gwynne finally put down her needle and sat beside her mother on her chaise longue near the fire. "You truly must not mind, Mama. Perhaps it was that Rhys and I were raised too much together. I would not have minded being his wife; I have always felt that it was my duty to be so, but haven't you always told Hu and me how you defied your family to marry Papa for love and how you hoped that neither of us would ever wed for any other reason?"

But her mother, though somewhat mollified, could not yet except the way events had turned. "But it is not as if there were *no* loving or liking between you," she said, dabbing at her eyes with a lace handkerchief. "It is not even as if there were some other young man who was ready to offer for you. It has always been such a settled thing between you and Rhys that we have never made the least push to find you a husband in the normal way. What on earth is to become of you?"

"Why nothing bad, of course." Gwynne patted her mother's hand reassuringly. "I love being with my family above all things and Papa has settled a generous amount on me so that I need never be dependent on anyone for my bread. It matters really very little to me if I have a husband or not. I think what I shall like most is becoming an aunt." She turned slightly to Bella, who returned her smile with a pleased one of her own.

"Oh!" said that young woman, rising with excitement. "I have it! I know exactly what you will do, Gwynne. Please say that you will."

"When I know what it is."

Bella turned to Hu. "I know you will not mind; in fact, I think you will like it very well." Before anyone could ask her to be plainer, Bella sat down, but her eyes held her joy and appeal. "Come with us to Cardiff. I mean live with us—forever if you wish it. After I am confined we will be coming here to live for a part of every year so you will not have time to miss your mama and papa and we would have such fun together, and you could help me with the baby as we had first planned, and maybe we will even find a husband for you and after all you might decide to give up being an aunt and become a mother yourself." She stopped, more because she had run out of breath than because she had run out of words.

Gwynne did not answer at once, and when she did, she replied to Hu not Bella. "Would you like the scheme? You must tell me if you would not."

"Of course I would," Hu said with an impatient wave of his hand. "I'm used to having you about here, aren't I?"

Gwynne appeared to find nothing daunting in this. "Mama? Would you spare me to Bella? The truth is that ever since I learned that Bella and Hu are to go to Cardiff for her confinement, I have been hoping that they would ask me to accompany them."

But Lady Madoc had already fastened on Bella's remark about the possibility of finding Gwynne a husband. Certainly living in the city and attending all the social events was much different from an occasional assembly; there was no reason at all to suppose that Gwynne had met and rejected or had been rejected by every eligible young man in the south of Wales. "I think it would be a delightful scheme," she said. "And I also think that in your last days, Bella, I shall come to you as well. Then when your baby is born, it will be almost like you had never left us."

Sir Thomas, who liked little fuss and had expected much from his wife over this, nodded happily. "I shall have Hu to stay with me immediately after. As likely as not you'll want him out from underfoot then in any case."

He looked to his son for confirmation of this but Hu only nodded abstractedly. Sir Thomas apparently noticed nothing unusual in Hu's unresponsiveness for the whole of the evening, nor did Gwynne or Lady

Madoc, but Bella cast her husband a brief anxious glance.

Catelyn still sitting apart from the others and virtually forgotten by them in their spate of planning, had the opportunity for observation of the company and noted this. She thought for the first time that Bella, for all her evident joy in her increasing condition, looked fretful. Catelyn had the idle thought that perhaps Hu was not taking well to the prospect of fatherhood and that this would quite naturally trouble his wife.

But the thought was fleeting, a minor distraction from the overwhelming news of the evening. She supposed she should support Gwynne in her plans, but just as she had been unable to offer the congratulations she had supposed she would have to offer this evening, for an entirely opposite reason she could not do this either.

It was very simple. Her heart was singing. Rhys was not to marry Gwynne and he hopelessly lost to her forever. It could not have been easy for him to be so honest with Sir Thomas and Gwynne; it had probably teased at the borderline of honor, a thing so much more understood by men than women, who regarded life as more important than mere ideas about it.

She could only wonder why. He might never have spoken at all; he might have been comfortable enough with Gwynne as his wife. There was only one reason she could think of, or rather only one reason she would allow herself to think of, that he wished to be free for her. She prayed fervently that this was the truth.

It was true that he had not actually asked her to be his, that their last meeting had been frought with anger and misunderstanding, but she found no discouragement in this now. When had she allowed him to openly declare himself? On the defensive because of his commitment to Gwynne and because she was so unsure of him and of her own feelings, she had been too busy attacking him to let him speak his mind. She reexamined every word they had said to each other since the moment he had kissed her at the Tremaine's ball and viewed all his behavior in a new light. She simply would not allow herself to believe anything other than that Rhys had chosen not to marry Gwynne because he was in love with her Cousin Catelyn.

This time, when next they met, she would hold her foolish tongue. She would allow no anxieties to make her say stupid things. Once again, her mercurial emotions were at high pitch and she supposed that she would have another sleepless night with her thoughts, but she found that unhappy anxieties are quite different from happy anticipation, and as the former had kept her awake now the latter lulled her to sleep.

15

When Catelyn awoke, she thought at first it must be morning, for she felt completely rested, but opening her eyes, she saw that the room was still in darkness. Though she heard nothing now, she realized it was a sound that had aroused her and her first thought was that Rhys had returned to their garden to court her once more as Captain Black. She sat up and threw back the sheets, ready to go to the window, when she heard the knock. She realized then that this was what she had heard.

Feeling a little disappointed, she quickly donned her wrapper and opened the door. To her astonishment, Bella stood on the other side of it. She was wearing a dressing gown over her night dress, but had on no slippers; she carried a bed candle and stood huddled as if cold, though the night was relatively balmy.

"Bella, what is it? Are you ill?" Catelyn touched the younger woman's arm to draw her into her room. When she closed the door, Bella responded by bursting into tears. Puzzled, but willing to offer Bella comfort, Catelyn led her over to the bed and sat them both upon it, cradling Bella in her arms.

"Oh, Cat, I am so frightened," Bella finally

managed to say when she could get her breath between sobs.

"Frightened? Whatever of?"

"Hu. Not of him, of course, for him. For me," she said disjointedly. Catelyn's experience with pregnant women was small, but she had heard that some were prone to anxiety and she assumed that this was the case with Arabella. She spoke soothingly and encouragingly and finally Bella became more calm. But when Bella was at last able to explain herself, Catelyn no longer doubted the reality of her fears.

"Hu thinks I don't know what he is about," Bella began. "I sleep very lightly and since I have been increasing, even more so. I heard him get up tonight and that first time a fortnight ago. The first time I said nothing because I thought he only wanted to go downstairs to read or for a glass of brandy to help him sleep. But it was hours before he returned, already dawn, and he moved about so much in his dressing room that I went in to see him. He smelled of horses."

Here she started to cry again and Catelyn thought she understood. Hu was riding off to meet a mistress, but in her condition, Bella didn't need to hear hard fact, she needed reassurance. "Perhaps he thought a bit of exercise would help him sleep," Catelyn suggested, and knew this sounded hopelessly stupid; he might walk as she had done, but who would choose to ride in the dark before dawn?

Bella shook her head sadly. "He was not surprised or disconcerted when I went into his room; he was furious. He was very defensive and told me that he was tired of me forever hanging on his coattails." She paused to swallow with difficulty. She had been looking down at the sodden handkerchief in her hands, but now she looked up at Catelyn, her lovely eyes red-rimmed and swollen. "I thought it must be another woman. I know Hu had mistresses before we were wed. I don't mind that and I know men sometimes stray—Mama warned me of it—but I could not disregard it simply because she told me I must."

"Because you love him."

"Yes, but I am still a little ashamed of what I have done." She placed her hand on Catelyn's arm for emphasis. Even in the light of the single candle, Catelyn could see how round her eyes were. "I have been positively eating myself up with jealousy and watching poor Hu for the least sign that would give him away, and a few days ago, I could not bear it another moment and I went into his room when I knew he would be out for some time with *beau-père.* I suppose I was hoping to find some note or token she had given him."

"Did you find anything," Catelyn asked. Bella only nodded and after a few moments Catelyn said, "What did you find?"

"A bag of new-minted guineas and another of mixed coin."

This was certainly not what Catelyn had expected to hear and for a few moments she did not comprehend. When she did, she could not have been more shocked. "Dear God," she said softly. "Are you certain?"

"Yes, of course." Arabella took a deep breath and went to the window. She seemed calmer now that the words were actually out. "I didn't understand at first. I know, for Papa has given me the hint, that from time to time Hu rides into Cardiff to visit a gaming hell. I have heard of this place and I know the stakes are high and fortunes are sometimes won and lost in a single day. I thought that must be it, but then the more I thought of it, the more I knew it could not be that."

She hugged herself tightly as if to prevent shivering and unknowingly looked down on the garden where Catelyn had met with Rhys as Captain Black. "I suppose I always knew what the money was, but oh, I could not bear to think of it."

Catelyn had not a doubt in the world about it. She nearly asked why Hu would do such a thing, but she already knew that answer and so did Bella. "I suppose he must owe a great deal of money, more than he dares to tell Sir Thomas or even me about," Bella said dully.

"Have you confronted him with what you have found?"

"I could not. He would be so angry with me for going through his things and learning such a thing about him." It was clear from her voice that she was about to begin crying again. "Now I wish that I had; no doubt it would have been worth it no matter what he said to me. It would have prevented him from doing it again, I am certain."

"Again?" Catelyn had come to the conclusion as Bella spoke that the highwayman she and Laurie had surprised on the road from Taff Wyd was Hu. No wonder he did not dare to stand up to them even though they were unarmed; he feared recognition. When that attempt was foiled, the robbery of Lord Tremaine's gold became necessary, but it made her suddenly cold inside to think that he would do it again. "Do you mean he has gone out again to rob someone?" she asked incredulously.

"I don't know it for certain," Bella said wretchedly, "but I think so. He got up tonight and dressed to go out just as he did before."

"He did this and you did not stop him?" Catelyn said, her voice breathless with amazement. "When did he go? How long is it since he left?"

"An hour perhaps. It took me awhile before I could think what I should do," Bella said.

"I think Sir Thomas did say something about Lord Tremaine sending out the wages again, thinking no one would suppose him to do it the same way again, but Hu cannot think they would not be prepared for the possibility of a second robbery." Catelyn spoke her thoughts aloud rather than actually addressing Bella. Arabella trembled quite visibly and ran to her side for reassurance.

"What will they do to him, Cat? They won't kill him! He doesn't really mean harm, I know it. Oh merciful God, what shall I do?" She once again broke into gulping sobs that quickly bordered on hysteria.

Catelyn continued to comfort her, but her soothing words were entirely mechanical; her mind was full of the thought of Hu posing as Captain Black and becoming a genuine highwayman. She knew that Hu was a selfish man, but to think of him holding up a cart at gunpoint was nearly impossible. He must indeed be desperate.

"What if they don't shoot him, but capture him? He will hang," Bella was saying, forcing Catelyn's thought to the most immediate problem. "Will they do that, Cat? Will they take him in charge?"

There were no comforting platitudes to answer this. "I don't know," Catelyn said honestly. "If he has been gone an hour, it is probably too late to do anything but wait and see what will happen."

"But we must do something. We must." Bella sounded desperate. "Please, Cat. Think of something."

With all of her heart, Catelyn wished for a solution to this latest coil. To think she had once thought country life dull! Even as they spoke the darkness seemed less heavy; it would be dawn in an hour or so. Catelyn considered saying that if Bella had confronted Hu before he left the house, they might not have this worry, but the young woman was completely overwrought and this was hardly the time to criticize her or expect her to think sensibly. Unbidden, yet another thought formed, or rather a longing. Catelyn wished she could put this burden into the hands of Rhys; she did not doubt his willingness or ability to deal with it. Even ignoring her feelings for him, she felt he should handle any difficulty that arose from his original masquerade, which, Catelyn could not doubt, had suggested the scheme to Hu. She also believed that putting the matter in his hands was tantamount to a solution.

But all these thoughts were nothing. A trembling, terrified Bella still sat beside her, murmuring disjointedly how they had to do something and even threatening to go after her husband herself. "Don't be absurd," Catelyn told her bracingly. "Where would you even know to go after him and in any case you do not ride well enough to consider this, especially in your condition."

"You do."

Catelyn was completely taken aback. "I? By myself? But how could I?"

"If you will not, I must."

Catelyn attempted to dissuade Bella from this stance, but she could not be moved. Nor could she be persuaded to go to Sir Thomas and tell him, for she could not bear to see Hu so cast down in his father's eyes.

Catelyn had no intention of riding alone into the middle of a highway robbery, but even less did she intend to allow the highly emotional Bella to do this. She said this and Bella rose, oblivious to all logic. "Very well, then. I shall go. You can't stop me."

Bella walked to the door, and Catelyn knew the choice was not hers. "I'll do it, Bella," she said resignedly. "But you must not expect too much."

Bella was overjoyed. She helped Catelyn to dress and all the while suggested arguments she was certain would bring Hu to his senses and cause him to return home at once. Pulling on her riding gloves and picking up her beaver riding hat and crop, Catelyn said tartly, "The mere sight of me, if he does not take fright and shoot me from my horse, will put an end to the thing, I should think. I would be better served if you will tell me what I am to say to the groom when I ask him to saddle a horse for me at this hour."

But surprisingly, that proved no difficulty. The stables were already stirring when Catelyn entered, and though groom looked mildly startled, he did as she bid without question—he was becoming quite used to the young woman and her unusual requests. An oblique inquiry made her reasonably certain that no horses had been taken out of the stables, but at this time of year a number of horses were left out in the pastures overnight and it would be an easy enough task to saddle one without anyone being aware of it. Come dawn, though, there would be an informal head count, so Hu had to be back very soon after sunrise if he was to avoid detection.

As she gathered up her reins and brought her somewhat skittish mount under her control, she fully expected to achieve no more than a very early morning ride. She did not know the estate well enough to take unfamiliar paths and she doubted very much that Hu would do his traveling where he might be readily seen, but she had promised Bella and she dutifully started off down the drive, turning, when she reached the road, in the direction of Cardiff.

The sky was beginning to lighten and no other soul was stirring. All she heard was her own horse trotting on the road. In this nearly complete silence, she suddenly heard rustling in the brush beside her. She was not aware of her nervousness until she started at the noise, giving her horse fright and causing him to shy. She held her seat, but her heart beat rapidly.

Catelyn heard the rustling again and her horse let out a soft whicker, which was almost instantly responded to by another horse. Moving on instinct rather than sense, she urged her horse to enter the bushes and a little way on, near a large clump of brush, she found the horse, fully bridled and saddled but riderless, the reins trailing on the ground. The horse came up to meet them in a friendly way and Catelyn recognized it as one from the Madoc stable.

Though her fright was over, her heart was still pounding. She dismounted and tethered both horses, walking further into the thick brush of the wood to search for the missing rider. Hu was lying on his face in a patch of bramble, his head perilously near a large rock. He made no move or sound at her approach, and when she stooped over him, her heart was in her mouth. But he was breathing quite normally, it seemed to her. There were scratches on his face and hands, but he seemed otherwise uninjured.

A chill of horror went through Catelyn and she quickly turned him over but found no sign of a pistol wound. She sighed in relief. For some reason Hu had fallen or been thrown from his horse, no doubt striking his head on the rock but without the force to break the skin. She could only assume that the stunning was temporary and that he would soon return to consciousness, but she could not be certain. Neither could she be certain whether or not he had accomplished his purpose, but if there had been any lingering doubts at what that purpose had been, they vanished at the sight of him. He was dressed in a black greatcoat she did not recognize and a battered black tricorn hat lay near to him. A search of his pockets revealed an opera mask doubtless taken from one of the ladies of the house. He had obviously changed his costume from the one she and Laurie had seen to tie his crimes to the legend of Captain Black.

Catelyn had no idea what to do with him. She simply could not leave him, but neither could she return to Madoc to fetch aid. Given the recent events, there would have to be talk among the servants when he was found at such a time and place and dressed in such a way. She even wondered if she could bring him to consciousness herself.

Catelyn did not have her vinaigrette, and if there was water nearby, she had no idea where. But before these problems could tax her further a much greater one appeared. She heard the sound of approaching horses and once again felt a pang of fear in her stomach. She quickly went over to the horses, hoping her presence would keep them quiet; she was reasonably certain they could not be seen from the road.

As the travelers drew near, she heard men's voices, and when they passed her, she imagined she heard the name of Captain Black spoken, though she could not absolutely convince herself that her own nerves had not conjured the sound. Once again a longing came over her to put this all in the hands of Rhys.

Catelyn could not say why she assumed he would help her and that it would be safe for her to trust him; she simply knew it, and truly, it was the only choice she had.

The same difficulties in going to him the day before existed now, but the situation was more desperate. Decided on this, she did what she could to make Hu comfortable, gathering up a cushion of leaves for his head and laboriously dragging him half under a bush to avoid casual detection. His horse was the greater problem, and in the end, when she had remounted her own horse with some difficulty because of her trailing habit, she simply brought the other in tow.

When she rode up to the front door of Llanbryth, her courage nearly failed her. But she took herself in hand and boldly rang the bell. She full expected to have to do this more than once at this early hour, but the door was opened nearly at once by the butler Thymes.

Catelyn also expected to have a long wait for Rhys, who would first have to be roused from his bed and dress, but he came to the saloon where she awaited him in only a very few minutes, and he too was dressed for riding.

He saw at once that she was distressed. "You are alone? Has something happened at Madoc?"

"No, but something *is* the matter," she said flatly, rising as he entered. "It is Hu; he is in the gravest trouble, and though I suppose I have no right to ask it of you, I could think of no one else to turn to for help."

"I am honored," he said quietly and tonelessly. "But if Hu is in trouble, why doesn't he come to me?"

If Catelyn had told her incredible story to almost

any other man of her acquaintance, including members of her own family, they would have assumed she was blowing things out of proportion. In fact, she fully expected, when she finished, a barrage of doubts and questions, but she was wrong.

"How far is he from here?" he asked at once.

"Less than a mile, but it is to the east and so close to the road that I fear someone may find him quite by accident, or that he may regain consciousness and stumble onto the road himself."

"Where is his horse?"

"I brought it here. It is outside. I think your butler thought it most odd, but I couldn't explain so I didn't even try."

Rhys smiled faintly. "The vagaries of the quality," he said succinctly. "They all think we are half mad, you know. Would a sane woman pay a morning call at sunrise in the first place?"

Catelyn responded with a smile and realized that despite their last meeting and although she still did not know his heart and mind—or he hers—there was ease between them.

As if they were about to embark on a planned ride, he led her outside and assisted her onto her horse and then mounted Hu's. Both of them were silent, but not uncomfortably so. The distance was short, but a cart passed them and later a neighbor on horseback, and Catelyn was reminded again how each passing minute made the situation more dangerous. At least no one stopped them with news of a further robbery or a hunt for a highwayman.

Hu was still where she had left him but was already stirring and moaning. Catelyn was first from her horse and quickly knelt beside him. His eyes opened and he blinked at her as if she were a stranger. Then he saw

Rhys, who had dismounted and come to kneel beside her. "What the devil is this?" Hu asked, his voice thick.

"What the devil, indeed," Rhys said grimly. He assisted Hu into a sitting position and, at the latter's insistence, helped him to rise to his feet. Hu swayed alarmingly, but grasping at his friend and at a tree next to him for support, he managed to remain upright. "I must have gone off my horse; I don't remember. How are you here?"

"Cat found you and came for me." Rhys then suggested dryly that since the day was rapidly warming, Hu might wish to remove the greatcoat.

Hu seemed surprised that it was on and said, "When I came out for my ride this morning it was surprisingly chill and . . ."

"Cut line, Hu," Rhys advised him curtly. "I know why you were out this morning and so does Catelyn. It won't help matters to deny what you've been about and we shall need all of each other's cooperation if we are to get out of this coil with your neck."

Hu's attempt at injured dignity was sadly flat. "I have no idea what you mean," he said with no conviction at all in his voice.

"Can you ride?" Rhys asked, completely ignoring this. "It would be best, I think, if you were to come with Cat and me to Llanbryth to be cleaned up and for us to decide what we are to say and do next."

"I know what I am doing next," Hu said stubbornly. "I am going home to Madoc." He cast off Rhys's support and started toward his horse, but he had only gone one step when his face contorted and he crashed heavily to the ground.

Catelyn at once went to her knees beside him. "He is unconscious again," she said worriedly.

"I think he has just fainted," replied Rhys, who was examining Hu's legs. "His ankle may be broken and I think the pain of this and his head injury made him go out again. It complicates the matter further, but in a way it is best. Do you think you could hold his horse very steady while I put him over the saddle?"

Catelyn did so. Though he moved more freely, Rhys's injured arm made lifting Hu into the saddle no easy work, but at last the task was done and they began to wend their slow way to Llanbryth. They remained in the wood far enough from the road to avoid detection until Rhys judged that they were near enough to the entrance of his estate. Fortune smiled on them and they encountered no one at all. They returned to the house through the garden entrance to avoid curious servants, Rhys carrying Hu as best he could from his horse into the house, then dropping him with relief onto the sofa.

In a short while, Hu was again awake and sitting up. He was protesting vigorously Rhys's suggestion that they cut away his boot to look at his ankle. "There's not a damn thing the matter with me but a bit of a sprain and the wind knocked out of me. I don't know why you are trying to make something out of an early morning ride. Female hysteria, I suppose. No doubt Bella noticed I'd gone out and started imagining things. Cat was easy enough to convince, I imagine, but I should have thought better of you, Rhys."

Neither Catelyn nor Rhys answered this and Hu took umbrage at their exchanged glance. "Next I suppose you'll be saying it was me posing as Captain Black and holding up Tremaine's cart and making up to Cat in the garden." He said this quite nastily. "I warn you, Cousin, you had better not be putting ideas like that in Bella's head."

But Catelyn was not bothered by his poor attempts to save face. "Oh, I *know* that it was not *you* in the garden, Hu," she said with a credible imitation of his usual condescending smile.

Hu flushed angrily and once again started to rise and once again was overcome by pain. "Since you have no choice but to sit there, Hu," Rhys said levelly, "I think you had better know you are only wasting our time in this pretense. You should not be attacking Catelyn; if it were not for her, someone quite different would have found you this morning, and like as not, you'd be in jail in Cardiff by now."

Briefly, and brooking no interruption, Rhys recounted the morning's events. "So you see, nothing you could say would convince either of us of your innocence," he finished. "The best thing is to let us help you. Frankly, I am not sure you are worth the bother, but I owe a great deal to your family and would like to avoid a scandal such as this would be."

Hu's expression was still mulish, but then he looked away from them and buried his face in his hands. "That's the damned thing about marriage; a man is hardly his own person anymore. Who the devil told Bella to go searching in my room?"

"If you had not behaved suspiciously and made her doubt you, she would not have done so," Catelyn said, having no intention of allowing him to malign his wife, who she felt loved him better than he deserved.

"I suppose you picked up upon and expanded that rumor of the guard hitting and wounding the highwayman so that no one would think to connect you with the crime," Rhys said to him. "It was unwitting, I suppose," he added dryly, "but that has caused me a deal of unnecessary pain. In one way or another, Hu, you have made us all suffer for your crimes."

Hu had no reply to this, but he hung his head so abjectly that it was clear that some of his spirit had left him, and Rhys took this opportunity to ring for the things he needed to see to Hu's injury.

16

Thymes himself came at his master's summons. He had not even been aware of Lord Trefor's return, and when he came into the room and saw them all, he betrayed the intensity of his curiosity by no more than the flicker of a glance directed at Catelyn and Hu.

A note was dispatched at once for Arabella, which was as reassuring and discreet as possible. Strong scissors, cold compresses, and bandage strips were brought to the study, and over Hu's constant complaint, Catelyn and Rhys removed the boot from his foot and tended to the ankle, which did not appear broken after all.

Instead of being grateful to his rescuers, Hu cursed them for every little pain and never uttered a word of thanks. By the time his foot had been bound and he had been dosed with brandy, Catelyn was fully prepared to give him the lecture on selfishness and moral turpitude he deserved.

She got as far as a pithy comment on ingratitude when a touch on her arm from Rhys gave her pause. His eyes bade her be silent, but there was something more in their expression that not only made her obey but made her heart flutter in her breast like a captive bird.

She had come to Rhys for his help, but it had been with some trepidation. Not a great deal of conversation had passed between them since her arrival at Llanbryth, certainly nothing private, but she realized with a sudden lightening of her mood that it was unnecessary. They seemed to know the wishes of each other without speaking.

Catelyn was a little afraid of the joyful excitement she felt building inside of her. In spite of her hope and happiness that he was not to marry Gwynne, he had never actually spoken to Catelyn herself of love. Yet the tenderness in his eyes when he looked at her, the very strength of her own feelings, which he himself had told her could not be so strong and be unreciprocated, gave her encouragement. He could not speak to her now, of course, but she had hoped that he would. Hu still fussed and made himself thoroughly unpleasant, but now she barely noticed.

It was a full three-quarters of an hour from the time Rhys had dispatched the note to Madoc Hall before Bella and Sir Thomas arrived, but Catelyn's patience with her difficult cousin never wavered.

It was obvious from the moment they entered the room that Bella had told all to her father-in-law. Sir Thomas looked deflated. Even his usually erect posture sagged and his eyes bespoke his sadness and disappointment in his son and heir.

As soon as Bella came in, she ran across the room and cast herself upon Hu, sobbing and repeating his name. Catelyn half expected Hu to castigate his wife for her prying then and there, but he forebore—at least for now—and was quite kind to her except for a sharp word when she inadvertently touched his injured leg.

Sir Thomas's eyes fell upon the greatcoat and

tricorn, which Rhys had tossed over a nearby chair. "Then it is true?" he said, addressing Rhys.

"I am afraid so, sir," Rhys said gently.

Sir Thomas sat heavily in the nearest chair. "Is it as Bella believes, Hu? Do you have gaming debts that you would not wish me or her to know of?"

"Yes," said Hu with no further attempt at subterfuge. "And there was a woman as well." This elicited a groan from his wife, who was beside him on the sofa. "I'm sorry, Bell, but there's no point in lying anymore. Glynnis thought I'd marry her, and when I wed you instead, she began doing all in her power to make my life hell.

"I thought I had the thing settled," he said with a glance at Rhys, which that man alone understood, "but she has had a child which she claims is mine though I don't believe her. I preferred to pay her rather than have her come to you or my father. We never would have had the Cardiff house, Bella, if your father had wind of this."

"So you thought the solution was to steal the money," his father said roughly.

"No, but I was desperate and wasn't thinking."

"Yet you went out again this morning apparently bent on doing it again."

"No," said Hu, and so forcefully that he made Bella beside him jump. "That is, I did mean to do it. I needed only a few hundred more guineas to meet the amount Glynnis was demanding of me and to pay off the last of my debts. Then I would have been clear of that mess forever. I didn't want to do it again, but the first time I failed completely and the second didn't bring me enough. But when I was along the edge of the road and I heard the cart coming toward me again, I just couldn't do it. I was afraid they would be ready for me this time." He seemed unaware of the damage he did to his own character by admitting that fear for his own neck had mattered more than the seriousness of the crime he had intended to commit.

"You were quite right," said his father, lowering his head into his hands in a gesture of dejection similar to the one Hu had used earlier. "Tremaine hired two extra armed men this time. My God," he added as if the realization had only just struck him, "my son a highwayman."

"Thank God Hu came to his senses," Bella said. "When neither of you came back, I was nearly hysterical. I did not want to tell anyone, truly, but I was all but convinced that you had somehow both been killed. I had to tell *beau-père.*" With a sudden change of expression, she asked, "Where is Laurie?" and Catelyn realized that she had not even noted that young man's absence until now.

"Mercifully asleep, I make no doubt," said his brother. "It takes an earthquake to shake him from his bed most days. It is as well, the fewer people who must know the truth of this the better."

"I don't see how that is to be prevented," said Sir Thomas, sounding as wretched as he looked. "Hu can't keep the money, whatever the consequences of returning it."

"And you cannot have that scandal attached to your name and your son hanged as a common thief," said Rhys. "You are upset, sir, and not thinking. We will find a way to return the money privately and quietly. I am afraid that I think it something of a pity that Hu should come out of this so unscathed, but there is no help for it. It might not be a terrible idea for him to squarely face his debts and this young woman who is blackmailing him."

Sir Thomas gave a short nod of agreement. "Given

what I have learned here today, I think it would be a great mistake for Hu to have his own establishment in Cardiff. He and Bella will decline her father's generous offer and will continue to live at Madoc Hall, where Hu will learn to conduct himself properly as one of his station in life."

There was no response to this from Hu or even from Bella, who was as affected by this pronouncement as her husband.

Rhys had his traveling carriage brought around to convey Hu home in comfort and he and Catelyn went with the Madocs to the front courtyard to see him comfortably installed within it. Sir Thomas was to ride back alone in the gig, which had brought him and Bella to Llanbryth; the horse Hu had ridden would be brought over later to Madoc by one of Rhys's grooms, and Catelyn insisted that she preferred to ride home on the horse she had ridden.

Bella was riding in the carriage with her husband, but before she entered, she hugged Catelyn warmly. "Thank you," she said with feeling. "Hu and I owe all our happiness to you."

"I did very little," said Catelyn. "And what I did do was the result of luck more than effort."

"If you had not gone after Hu when I asked you, someone else might have found him. I know this and so does Sir Thomas, and so, I think, does Hu," she added, casting a glance at her husband, who was lying still across the seat with his eyes closed. "Only, I don't expect he will admit it."

"I am sorry for you, Bella," Catelyn said. "I know how excited you were about living in Cardiff again and being near your parents."

The younger woman shrugged. "I wanted it as much for Hu as for myself. But I see now that it might not be a good thing. And we can still stay there part of the year with my parents. I know he dislikes this because he thinks my papa smells of the shop, but if he does not care to come with me and our child when we visit, he is welcome to remain at Madoc." Her chin lifted slightly in promise of her future defiance of her husband.

Catelyn only hoped that she would continue in this. She did not believe that a man was entitled to rule absolutely over his wife, whatever the law might say. The saddest part of it, though, was that so many women like Bella would gladly submit to this power if men did not abuse it, and most men did not even realize it. She gave Bella's hand a reassuring squeeze and only wished that she might still be about to support her.

Catelyn and Rhys remained outside until the carriage disappeared around a bend in the drive. The silence between them began to lengthen and for the first time Catelyn felt awkward with him.

"I had best leave as well," she said, but hoped he would dissuade her.

"Have you had any breakfast today?" he asked, and she could only smile at the practical, unromantic question, so different from what she had been hoping for.

She wished him to make violent love to her and he concerned himself only with her stomach. Oddly this endeared him to her. "No," she said. "But I am sure that Aunt Bess will have something prepared against our arrival. After that I think I shall be self-indulgent and sleep away the afternoon."

He smiled slightly. "That sounds like the behavior of the creature after which you are called. Have you ever thought it a pity that your eyes are not green instead of blue? It would be more fitting for a 'cat,' don't you think?"

And this nonsense made her love him all the more. "No," she said, laughing.

He took her hand in his. "Have breakfast with me. Laurie should be up by now and will join us soon."

Catelyn agreed, but hoped that Laurie would not be too quick in coming downstairs.

He led her to the breakfast room, which was on the same side of the house as the study and received the morning sun. Though she chided herself for counting her chickens, she could not help the thought that she would like to break her fast each morning in this cheery room. He rang for the footman and breakfast was laid out at once. She was a light eater in the morning, but he would not hear of her having nothing but chocolate and toast and piled her plate with eggs and ham and cast the eye of a parent over her while she ate.

But Catelyn was able to do scant justice to the food when her mind was so much elsewhere. She could not bear it another minute and finally said baldly, "Why did you not marry Gwynne?"

He seemed surprised by the question. "Did you not hear the whole of it? She did not especially wish to marry me."

"I did hear the whole of it," she said, "and I know that the easiest course for you would have been simply to offer for Gwynne if you had no other inclinations. But you did not."

"No I did not."

Infuriatingly, most of his attention was being given to his plate, but a brief glance sent her way showed her the laughter behind his bland expression. "You are laughing at me," she said with mock indignation.

"A little," he admitted with no sheepishness at all.

"You have always been laughing at me, haven't you? I should hate you."

At these words, she had his complete attention. He put down his fork and turned to her. "Do you?" There was no amusement in his expression now.

"No," she admitted very softly.

He got up, went around the table, and gave her his hand to rise. "I am devilish sharp-set, but I fear the food will have to wait." He cast a baleful eye at the table. "There is something daunting about a table covered with eggs when one wishes to make love."

Catelyn felt the warmth of his touch. If any last doubts lingered in her mind about whether or not she would respond to him in the way that she had responded to Captain Black, these were removed forever. "Is that what you wish to do?"

"Yes. Is it what you wish?"

"Yes." The word was barely spoken before she found herself in an embrace that was almost fierce. But in spite of his intensity, he was gentle, and she knew that when the heat of their passion finally cooled, the coals would be merely banked and not spent.

When he released her, she caught sight of the full table beside them and laughed. "You are right, it is too much to expect the practical to exist in perfect harmony with the romantic. We had better either have our meal and be romantic later or give the food up in the name of love."

He knew she was teasing, but nobly he did not rise to the bait. "I find after all that the one hunger is not nearly as potent as the other," he said, and they then went across the hall to a small saloon.

They found a small sofa near the windows and embraced as soon as they were on it. But after a time she gently pushed him away. "Longing for your kippers, are you?" he said sadly.

She would not succumb to his nonsense. "Why were you so cruel to me yesterday when I came here? You must have known that I came here because I wanted to tell you that I was surprised and confused by our conversation at the Tremaines' and did not then know my heart."

"I guessed. No, that is too arrogant. I hoped. But what could I say to you, Cat. 'I love you but there exists the possibility that I may have to marry someone else.' I had to settle the matter with Gwynne and her family first."

"Would you have married her if she held you to it?"

He was holding both her hands in his. He looked down at them for a long moment before answering. "I don't know if I could have. I thank God I did not have to make that choice. To be honest, I am quaking in my boots at the thought that I shall now have to tell Sir Thomas that it is his niece that I wish to marry. Perhaps I shall travel to London instead and wait on your father directly."

"You don't have to," she told him. "Papa is coming here tomorrow or the next day. I wrote to him and asked him if I could come home."

"To escape certain ravishment by Captain Black?"

"To escape wishing to be ravished by him," she said with brutal honesty.

This was nearly accomplished, for once again Catelyn found herself enfolded in his strong arms. It was in this pose that Laurie found them.

"Smelling of April and May," he said with relish when he saw them. "I knew how it would be."

"If you are that perceptive," said his brother, "then you will know what I now wish."

Laurie shook his head with a smile. "What is it?"

"That you would go and find your breakfast."

"I'm not especially hungry."

Rhys sighed. "Then go and tell Thymes that I wish a

message sent around to Madoc telling them that Cat will be delayed."

"You don't need me for that, just pull the bell."

"I fear you are sadly *unperceptive*, dear brother."

But Laurie's smile was teasing. "It occurs to me that if you are to marry an heiress, I ought to bargain for a better allowance."

"If you do not leave us, you may have to bargain for one at all."

Laurie smiled again at this, but not one to take chances, he at last left the happy couple alone.

About the Author

Originally from Pennsylvania, Elizabeth Hewitt lives in New Jersey with her husband and cat. She enjoys reading and history, and is a fervant Anglophile. Music is also an important part of her life; she studies voice and sings with her church choir and with the New Jersey Choral Society. THE FORTUNE HUNTER was written to a background of baroque music, as were her two previous novels for Signet's Regency line, BROKEN VOWS and A SPORTING PROPOSITION.

HOW TO WRITE A ROMANCE AND GET IT PUBLISHED

Updated Edition
by Kathryn Falk,
publisher of *Romantic Times*

Intimate advice from the world's top romance writers:

JENNIFER WILDE · BARBARA CARTLAND · JANET DAILEY · PATRICIA MATTHEWS · JUDE DEVERAUX · BERTRICE SMALL · JAYNE CASTLE · ROBERTA GELLIS · PATRICIA GALLAGHER · CYNTHIA WRIGHT

No one understands how to write a successful, saleable romance better than Kathryn Falk. Now she has written the best, most comprensive guide to writing and publishing romance fiction ever—for both beginners and professionals alike. From the field's top writers, agents, and editors come tips on:

- FINDING THE FORMULA: ROMANCE RULES
- SELECTING A GENRE: FROM HISTORICALS TO TEEN ROMANCE
- LISTINGS OF PUBLISHING HOUSES, EDITORS, AGENTS
- WRITING SERIES AND SAGAS
- THE AUTHOR-AGENT RELATIONSHIP
- ADVICE FOR MEN, HUSBANDS, AND WRITING TEAMS

Coming in January From Signet

SIGNET REGENCY ROMANCE
COMING IN NOVEMBER 1989

---·---

Mary Jo Putney
Carousel of Hearts

Emily Hendrickson
The Gallant Lord Ives

Evelyn Richardson
The Education of Lady Frances

---·---

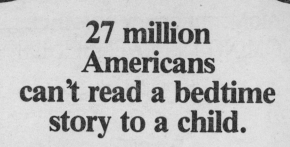

27 million Americans can't read a bedtime story to a child.

It's because 27 million adults in this country simply can't read.

Functional illiteracy has reached one out of five Americans. It robs them of even the simplest of human pleasures, like reading a fairy tale to a child.

You can change all this by joining the fight against illiteracy.

Call the Coalition for Literacy at toll-free **1-800-228-8813** and volunteer.

Volunteer Against Illiteracy. The only degree you need is a degree of caring.